SHE WAS AN INMATE WIFE UNTIL
HE DID HER WRONG.

PRISON
THRONE

T. STYLES

NATIONAL BEST SELLING AUTHOR OF *RAUNCHY*

Styles

Library of Congress Control Number: 2014938741

ISBN 10: 0989790142

ISBN 13: 978-0989790147

Cover Design: Davida Baldwin www.oddballdsgn.com
Editor(s): T. Styles, C. Wash, S. Ward
www.thecartelpublications.com
First Edition
Printed in the United States of America

Library of Congress Cataloging-in-Publication Data

Styles, Toy, 1974-
    Prison throne / by T. Styles. -- First edition.
        pages cm
    ISBN 978-0-9897901-4-7 (pbk. : alk. paper)
1. Man-woman relationships--Fiction. 2. Drug traffic--Fiction. I. Title.

PS3619.T95P85 2014
813'.6--dc23

                              2014015785

15.00
2/23/16
DS

114140706

ARE YOU ON OUR EMAIL LIST?

CHECK OUT OTHER TITLES BY
THE CARTEL PUBLICATIONS

What's Up Fam,

I know most of you still have your mouths open from reading, "Silence of The Nine". I feel you, that novel was on another storytelling level. If you haven't read it yet, do yourself a huge favor and grab it today. I'm dead ass! (Serious)

Now, get ready to have your mouths open some more. The book on deck, "Prison Throne", has to be T. Styles's **GREATEST** love story written so far. This joint crashes into the heart and at times leaves you breathless. I felt the love and emotions between Rasim and Snow but I couldn't deny feeling the pain either. That's what unconditional love is all about. Trust me, you gonna go through it with this one, but you not gonna put it down until the last page.

Keeping in line with tradition, we want to give respect to a vet or trailblazer paving the way. With that said we would like to recognize:

Karen E. QuinOnes Miller

Karen E. Quinones Miller is the veteran author of such classic stories like, "Satin Doll"; "Using What You Got"; "Uptown Dreams"; "Satin Nights"; "I'm Telling"; "An Angry Ass Black Woman"; as well as, "Harlem Godfather: The Rap on My Husband, Ellsworth "Bumpy" Johnson", which she co-authored with the late Mayme H. Johnson. Karen has been penning great novels for well over a decade and The Cartel Publications supports her work completely. Make sure you do the same and check her out.

Aight, without further adieu, I'ma let you go ahead and dive

in! Enjoy yourself and I'll get at you in the next novel.
Be Easy!
Charisse "C. Wash" Washington
Vice President
The Cartel Publications
www.thecartelpublications.com
www.facebook.com/publishercwash
Instagram: publishercwash
www.twitter.com/cartelbooks
www.facebook.com/cartelpublications
Follow us on Instagram: Cartelpublications

Dedication

I dedicate this book to the City of Philly. You have been
tried and true from the beginning of my career.
I love you.

Acknowledgements

I acknowledge all of my fans around the world. I'm a
better writer because of you.

MAY I SUGGEST A PLAYLIST?

These songs stayed on rotation during the creation of PRISON THRONE.

I hope you enjoy them.

1. B.A.N.S – Sevyn Streeter
2. Primetime (Feat. Miguel) – Janelle Monae
3. Just To Keep You Satisfied – Marvin Gaye
4. 4 AM – Melanie Fiona
5. Tender Love – Force M.D.'S
6. On Bended Knee – Boyz II Men
7. Roller Coaster – Toni Braxton & Babyface
8. I Don't Like Me – K. Michelle
9. Can't Raise A Man – K. Michelle
10. FYH – TGT
11. Love And War – Tamar Braxton
12. I Never Wanna Live Without You – Mary J. Blige
13. You're All I Need (Feat. Mary J. Blige) – Method Man
14. Ghetto (Feat. Yo Gotti) – August Alsina
15. Kissin' On My Tattoos – August Alsina
16. I Luv This Shit (Remix) – August Alsina
17. Mine (Feat. Drake) – Beyonce

DEAR READER,

MY FAMILY AND I WOULD LIKE TO THANK

YOU FOR PURCHASING MY BOOK.

I AM FOREVER GRATEFUL.

- T. STYLES

PROLOGUE

MAY 2014
WASHINGTON, DC
PRESENT DAY

Instead of May flowers eighteen SWAT officers with automatic assault weapons dressed the front lawn of the brick house in northeast Washington, DC. All were prepared to hold court in the streets if the terrorist inside so desired. It was totally up to him; well, for the moment anyway.

Rookie hostage negotiator Alf Herman, who wished to be called by his first and middle name, slogged slowly toward the concrete steps leading up to the property with his hands raised high in the air. "I'm coming in!" he yelled, his heart less confident than his voice. "And I'm unarmed! Please don't shoot!"

There was a brief moment of silence, with the exception of the engines of the SWAT vehicles humming in the background.

"You had better be alone, cop," the Terrorist chided from inside the home. "I'm not fucking around!"

Alf Herman swallowed what was left of his valor and said, "I...I am!" His brown skin was reddening due to blood rushing to the surface of his face.

If bravery was a requirement, Alf would be out of his league. In fact, the closest he had ever come to a crime scene this gigantic was on his living room couch while

BY T. STYLES

watching the movie *Diehard*. Yet there he was, walking up the steps that could possibly lead to his demise.

Alf believed he was chosen for another reason and only he knew why.

Before he touched the knob leading into the premises, his stomach rumbled and he released bubbles of gas into the seat of his black slacks. He swallowed again and looked back at the men whose faces he couldn't recognize because they were veiled with black ski masks and helmets. He prayed they would be as vicious as they appeared if things got animated inside.

When he was as ready as he was going to be, he focused on the door and opened it slowly. Once inside, he saw what could only be described as a beautiful nightmare.

Broken glass was scattered along the powder white carpet and sparkled when kissed with the sunlight streaming through the shattered windows. Before him was a cherry wood staircase that could be accessed on either side of the foyer. At the very top were three closed doors and in front of the middle one was a bleeding body, which, from his vantage point, appeared to be a police officer.

Now Alf was horrified.

He assumed the Police Officer had been sent to meet his maker until he moaned.

"The...the man upstairs is still alive but he needs help," Alf announced as if the Terrorist didn't know. "Can I take him out and get him some help? Like you promised?" Because he could not see the Terrorist's face, he felt as if he were talking to the Wizard of Oz instead of a human being.

"There will be plenty of time for that," the Terrorist said, his voice so powerful that it vibrated the fragile bones in Alf's ear. "Right now I want you to take a seat!"

PRISON THRONE

There in the middle of the floor, as if it had suddenly appeared, sat a wooden chair. The rookie didn't see it before because he was focused on the carnage and despair.

"Please help me," the Police Officer moaned. "I feel weak."

"Shut the fuck up!" the Terrorist rebuked him. "You got everything you deserved, homie."

Trying to come to the man's rescue, thereby doing his job in the process, Alf gently said, "Please let me—"

Irritated with the cop for not following orders, Rasim's gun sounded off in the house, which caused the SWAT team to respond in kind by cocking their weapons. Everyone was speaking the same language now. War.

"Are you alright in there, Herman?" the lead SWAT officer yelled from outside of the house.

Alf was about to respond but the realization that the bullet could've been in his body gripped him like a scorned wife to her husband's balls. So when he opened his mouth to speak, instead of words coming out he vomited. The ham sandwich he consumed two hours earlier slapped against his left boot and stank terribly.

Aware that the only reason the house didn't look like a block of Swiss cheese after the Terrorist's dangerous move was because Alf was inside, he thought it smart to advise the SWAT Officer that he was okay. So he wiped his mouth with the back of his hand and yelled, "I'm fine!"

He could almost feel the officers outside relaxing. A little.

"Now that the show is over, have a seat, cop," the Terrorist importuned. "Bullets travel through wood so I won't ask again."

Wishing to get the matter over with quickly, Alf hustled toward the chair. Glass crackled under his boots as he moved forward. Since everything around him was salted with shards, and the chair was not, he assumed the seat was placed especially for him as if he were in VIP. At least it looked that way.

When he looked closer, he saw two dusty footprints. Who did they belong to?

He plunked into the chair and focused on the doors. "I'm seated!" He tried to turn off the tremble of his body but it was impossible.

"Good." The Terrorist paused. "Now I know this looks bad, cop. But I assure you that everything is not as it seems."

"Everything is exactly what it seems," a woman interrupted. She sounded disgruntled.

Alf's heartbeat quickened because he was not made aware that someone outside of the Terrorist and the cop was present.

"Who are you?" he asked as his eyes rolled over the three doors. He had no idea where anyone was located, which gave them the upper hand.

"I am Snow Nami."

He swallowed and wiped the sweat from his brow. "Snow, are you hurt?" he questioned as if he could do something about it if she were.

"Beyond understanding," she replied in a low voice.

"Don't play the martyr, Snow," the Terrorist responded. "This disaster is as much your fault as it is mine!"

She laughed as if she were taken to another place, like the front row of a comedy show. "You sound like a fool, nigga," she yelled. "Everything that's happening is your fault! A man who is not in control of his soul is a savage. And so are you!"

PRISON THRONE

PART ONE

BY T. STYLES

CHAPTER 1

RASIM NAMI
WASHINGTON, DC
APRIL 10, 1995

Hard rain slapped against the public bus's windows as sixteen-year-old Rasim shared a rear seat with Selena Amo, a seventeen-year-old strumpet. Her damp jean jacket was draped over their legs to hide his finger slithering into her drenched vagina.

Although the bus was crowded, Selena was totally with the shit. She didn't care who saw them or what they had to say. She was kicking it with Rasim, one of the cutest boys in high school. Besides, she had been crushing on him for the longest. The only complication was that Rasim didn't want a girlfriend. And if the truth be told, she was hoping the finger trip she allowed him to take inside her body would nudge him closer to being the relationship kind.

Occasionally Rasim would eye the bus driver from the large rearview mirror and ninety percent of the time he was looking in their direction. But all Rasim could do was hope he couldn't see his freak show.

A few passengers, who had as much going on in the bedroom as an empty bed, couldn't help but turn every so often to view the juveniles with distaste and pocketed envy.

The biggest offender was the older black woman sitting in front of him with a rat's nest on her head that was born a wig. The perfume she sported resembled the odor of a nasty stripper who attempted to conceal the stank of her pussy with cheap eau de toilette.

Every so often she would turn around, roll her eyes and threaten with her body language to get up and tell the driver. Neither teenager gave a fuck so after awhile she minded her own business.

When Selena's stop approached she piloted his wrist back and forth, in and out of her vagina until she squirted her cream over his fingertips. She did not want to leave until she got her rocks off. Satisfied, she moaned, bit down on her lower lip and looked over at him with a sly smile. "Ahhh, Rasim. That was nice. Thank you." She whipped her long, brown hair over her shoulder.

Having done little work, he didn't deserve the credit. But he smiled and kissed her pretty pink lips. Despite being a stone cold freak, Selena was a looker if she was nothing else. The kind of girl rappers would kill to have in their videos or on top of their dicks. A tiny mole sat on the tip of her nose and was not offensive in the least. In fact, Rasim found it quite twee.

In awe, she rubbed her hand over his smooth hair and down his soft cheek. She admired how handsome he was. Of pure Pakistani descent, his complexion was butter brown and his entire body was minus a blemish or flaw. He was scrawny, not a muscle in sight, but he was gorgeous to look at. "One day you and I will be forever connected," she predicted. "I can feel it in my heart."

Selena had the stage so he wouldn't counter her prediction although he didn't believe it. He wasn't trying to be with her for the long haul. Instead he pulled his hand out of her body. The air rushed against his wet digit until it stiffened due to being soaked with her icing. "I don't doubt it," he winked.

Selena buckled her jeans and looked out of the window. When she peeped familiar landmarks, she hopped up. Her sculpted buttocks brushed against his lips, on purpose of course, as she tugged the taut string to alert the driver. The bell rang and the bus slowed down as he approached the stop.

A photographer at heart, Rasim grabbed his Fuji disposable camera in preparation to take a flick or two of her physique. Rasim loved photography and when he took a photo you were pulled into it like a 3D experience.

As she waited, Rasim snapped a picture and looked her up and down. *Damn them jeans,* Rasim thought to himself. Her body was bubbly in the right places and he was thankful.

"You always taking pictures and shit," she grinned, loving the attention of her paparazzo.

"Maybe I like what I see."

Blushed, she whispered, "Bye, Rasim." She waved as if her fingers were playing a piano in the air.

"Later," he replied leaning back in his seat.

When the bus halted, she grabbed her jacket and tiny pink purse. Rasim stole another glimpse of her round ass and slim waist as she floated toward the back door. When it opened, she washed into the rain and the bus was back on its route again.

At first Rasim pretended he wasn't going to take a second look but he couldn't help himself. He leaned forward and watched as the rain painted her light blue jeans dark blue, revealing the red panties she was wearing in the process. He snapped a few more pictures for good measure and couldn't wait until he had them developed to show his boys. When he was done, he stuffed his camera into his book bag and thought about what he'd just done. Finger fucked the cutie.

The Latina mami was on point, no doubt, but there was one complication. The siren was simply too loose pussy for his taste. All of his friends took a ride on the beauty and when they were done, they essentially gave Rasim a transfer. Selena was frankly not the wifey type.

Remembering touching her plushness, he placed his fingers against his nose and inhaled deeply. Yep. At least she was fresh.

Now that the fun was over, it was time to get serious. So he dipped into his pocket and grabbed his crumpled white Kufi. As if it had never left his scalp, he slid it on his head so he wouldn't disappoint his parents when he got home.

Rasim's parents were Sunni Muslims and out of respect for his religion, he was persuaded to wear the Kufi to school by his father, whom he worshipped. Since, as far as he knew, the Kufi was not a requirement in their religion, he resented the accessory. Not only that, unlike his father, Rasim was born in America where those who were different were ridiculed. He didn't want to be Muslim or Pakistani. He wanted to be American more than he wanted to live and the Kufi contradicted that.

After Rasim pulled the cord to stop the bus, he grabbed his book bag and swaggered toward the backdoor and waited. Standing 6-foot 4-inches tall, the scrawny kid's head almost touched the roof of the bus.

When he glanced down, the old woman who hated on his game earlier observed his Kufi, which suddenly appeared, and frowned. The thin gray mustache she rocked, equal in color to her wig, gave her a hardened expression. "And you got the nerve to wanna showcase your religion now. What a disgrace to your God." She shook her head lightly back and forth, gripped the oversize brown purse in her lap against her knotty breasts and looked away.

Rasim was a cool kid and he felt sorry for her. He had a knack of sensing what a person felt in their heart as opposed to what they said or did.

Instead of getting angry at the old bird, when the bus stopped, he kissed the woman on the cheek and dipped down the stairs and out the door. He sensed that she was probably a sex-deprived woman who would never come in the company of a man like him again. So for a moment, he restored her youth.

As he stood at the stop outside, he could see the woman grinning and stroking the place he kissed as if she'd just won the lottery.

Mission accomplished.

When the charity was over, Allah seemed to smile down on Rasim because the rain ceased as he hustled down Rhode Island Avenue toward his house.

When he opened the door to his crib, he was about to stroll inside but stopped short when he saw Kamran, his father. He was standing with his back faced him while chanting rak'ah. Kamran was also turned toward Qibla for Salat (prayer). To face Qibla meant to turn in the direction of the Kaaba in Mecca.

Out of respect, Rasim closed the door softly and sat on the damp step to allow him privacy. He tossed his book bag next to him and looked out at the street. The echo of wet tires crawling down the road sounded off like soft music in the background. He loved the city.

His next-door neighbor, Bridget, who was sitting in her rocking chair on the porch, eyed him with disdain. She was a news whore who believed every negative thing she read about Muslim people.

Rasim waved and she jumped up, rolled her eyes and stormed inside. He had no beef with the old woman. In his mind, just like the woman on the bus, she was bitter and desired a more exciting life.

He shook his head, smiled and thought a lot about his own existence. Although he possessed good friends, Donald, Brooklyn and Chance, something was missing and he couldn't figure out what.

When he heard the door squeak, Rasim looked behind him and saw his father. Kamran inhaled the rain-scented air deeply, walked outside and sat next to his son. Gently, he touched him on his back and asked, "How was your day?"

Remembering Selena, he blushed and nodded, "Good. Very good."

Kamran considered his son's guileful grin and recognized it immediately. They were close and talked about everything. The twinkle in his eye was a dead giveaway and he knew something was up. "Let me smell your fingers," he joked.

Rasim giggled and allowed him access.

His father sniffed and said, "Ah, yes, this girl is fresh."

Rasim and his father erupted into heavy laughter.

"Yes, father, she is." He suppressed another chuckle.

Although their relationship was untraditional for some Muslim and Pakistani people, it worked for them. Kamran believed in allowing his son the room to be himself despite practicing the strict doctrine that he lived by as a Sunni Muslim daily. Because of his understanding of his son's needs in America, their bond was pure and intact.

As they simmered down, both men looked at the busy city zip by before their eyes. "Tell me, son, is this girl the marrying type?" he asked, going deeper.

Rasim exhaled. "No, father. Sadly, she is not. And I don't think I'll ever find that one who is."

"I doubt that very seriously," he responded. "You are a very handsome young man, Rasim. Why, women would give their first born to be with you." He chuckled.

"I don't think it's them. I think it's me. I haven't met anybody who is made for me."

Kamran's heart ached because he didn't want Rasim growing up without experiencing true intimacy. "Son, do not leave this world without knowing real love. It would be life's greatest shame."

When Umar Nami, Rasim's mother, walked outside, the door squeaked. Her body blocked the door from closing and she tucked her fists in her waist and looked down at her men. She knew they shared a bond resembling best friends as opposed to father and son and they often drove her mad. She wasn't hating and shit. She appreciated their close connection. She truly did. She just wanted to be sure that Kamran taught him the tough lessons to steer Rasim the right way too.

The pink hijab she wore was intended to hide her beauty, thereby keeping her modesty and morality in tact, but it failed drastically. Umar was so stunning that even with most of her face concealed, she was still pulchritudinous.

"What are you doing out here, Kamran?" She lowered her brow. "Smelling Rasim's fingers again?"

The men burst into laughter once more.

PRISON THRONE

The thing about the Nami family was this; they never took themselves too seriously. They were no different than a Christian family after worship was over. They believed in laughter and love to keep their family strong and it may not have worked for some but it did for them.

However, there was another reason Kamran strived for such a close fellowship with his son. He didn't have the benefit of his father when he grew up in Pakistan although he always desired him.

It was Vazir, his twin brother, who stepped up at the age of twelve to take on an active role in Kamran's life when their parents were murdered by a man who craved their father's paycheck and pressed a gun to the back of his head. Years later, Vazir married a rich woman and Kamran never saw him again.

"You two are going to give me a blue face," Umar said shaking her head. "Now go wash up." She paused. "And get your fingers good, Rasim," she said looking at her son. "Dinner is almost ready." She disappeared into the house.

Rasim stood up and helped his father up just as his friends Donald, Brooklyn and Chance were strolling up the block. He met Donald and Chance from his high school but Brooklyn came in his life another way.

The manner in which the teenage friends bopped toward the house closely favored a hip-hop group in a music video. When the four of them linked up, girls flocked just to be in their presence.

"Father, can I go with my friends?" Rasim asked as he looked at him with hopeful eyes.

Kamran looked at the young men, who in his opinion spelled trouble, and said, "Of course, son." He was a good father who knew in order for a man to grow, he must learn the lessons of the world. Kamran would never stand in Allah's way when he was in the process of teaching.

Rasim hugged his father, grabbed his book bag and immersed himself into the huddle of friends as if he were pulled into a tornado. They rocked all the way toward the car as if they hadn't a care in the world.

Kamran saw Rasim snatch off his Kufi and stuff it in his pocket. He lowered his head in shame. "Watch over him, Allah. He's all I got," Kamran whispered as he walked into the house.

The air conditioning was on blast and yet Donald Guzman was dripping with sweat. His ecru colored skin was riddled with both old and new scars as if he walked through a pile of cacti, face first. He always found a reason to fight and never walked away from a battle, yet Rasim looked up to him.

Donald provoked fear in everyone outside of his team. Although young, his name filtered throughout the streets of DC and he was feared by some and hated by others. He was a young boss who already held a hood throne. Donald was also Rasim's best friend and Rasim wanted to be just like him.

Powerful.

As they drove down the road toward a hotel to meet a business associate, something felt off with the mood so Rasim looked over at Donald. Rasim sat in the passenger seat of Donald's blue Acura Integra and wondered what demon possessed his best friend in the moment.

Was it the Demon of Desire that had him wanting to fuck any girl who allowed him? Often without protection? Or the Demon of Rage, which always caused him to act on his emotions violently for any reason he deemed necessary?

Whatever afreet held Donald's soul, Rasim hoped it wouldn't attack.

"I'm telling ya'll," Donald started as he piloted the car, "I'm sick of my folks. Every time I come home, they got the house smelling like old pussy 'cause they fucking some dirty ass couple in the living room like they can't go in the back and shit." He rubbed his forehead toward his hairline, taking some of the wetness with him.

"You already know how they are," Chance responded as he thumbed through the fifty-dollar bills in his wallet as if they would mutate into Benjamins, "they reliving their youth."

"Fuck that," Donald responded as he eyed him through the rearview mirror. "They supposed to be civilized and shit! They supposed to take care of they kids!"

"But you not no kid no more," Rasim kidded. "You a grown ass nigga."

Although Donald was angry, Rasim knew where his pain originated. His parents, Alonso and Paulino Guzman, Latinos from Baltimore City, indulged in guilt-free sex for most of his life. From ten-member orgies to public sex exploits, in an effort to bust a nut, they did it all. In fact, his parents met at a swingers party although Paulino came with another man and his father came with another woman. They realized they were more compatible and had been together ever since.

Pregnancy was never for the Guzmanes. In the earlier days, Paulino was good with taking birth control since condoms were out of the question for Alonso. But when cocaine enrolled itself into their lives after awhile she was too horny to take the pill and eventually Donald was born.

When Donald was a week old, the couple played it cool and renounced all erotic activity. That was until Alonso woke up with a hard on one day that couldn't be satisfied despite the four lovemaking sessions he and Paulino accomplished earlier. It was clear that although they were new parents, his dick had other intentions.

So they dropped the baby off at Paulino's parents' house and before long Donald had become a regular fixture in his grandparents' home. A few packed diaper bags here and a new outfit there were the most Donald got from his parents and his loneliness turned to resentment and stopped abruptly at anger.

"You think I don't know I'm not a kid no more?" Donald asked Rasim, his eyes twirling around slightly. His demeanor was giving, *Please say something wrong so I can push your teeth toward the back of your scalp.*

Oh, it was the Demon of Rage that chose to visit and unfortunately for Rasim, he was in the front seat.

Rasim didn't partake in violence. Besides, he was the jokester of the crew. The one his friends called on when they wanted to chuckle their troubles away. A gangster he was not and, as far as he knew, a gangster he would never be.

"Not trying to get you mad, man," Rasim said flashing the winning smile he was known for. He nudged him softly on the arm. "Chill out and stop tripping."

Donald took another look at Rasim, blinked a few times and called the demon off. He had beef in the streets but it was never with Rasim. He loved him more than a brother. "Ain't nobody mad at your bitch ass," Donald lied.

"You ain't mad?" Rasim repeated. "Your face so wet you making my dick hard," he laughed.

Donald shook his head and chuckled at his friend.

On some personal shit, Brooklyn pulled on Donald's headrest to scoot forward, which caused Donald's head to lean back abruptly. Donald hated that shit.

"How far are we from the hotel? I'm hungry," he asked with his lips too close to Donald's ear.

"Nigga, get the fuck off of my seat!" he yelled. "And we 'bout ten minutes out." He paused. "Stop being so fucking greedy. That's why your neck beefy as is. You eat too fucking much."

Embarrassed, he flopped back in the seat and rubbed his coffee colored chin. "Fuck you," he said under his breath. When Chance and Rasim laughed too he continued, "Fuck all you niggas."

What Donald said was true. Brooklyn's body inflated weekly and if it hadn't been for his cute face and five o'clock shadow, he would've had a problem in the ladies department.

Unlike some wannabes who sought street cred by claiming Brooklyn, he was a true transplant from the city that never slept. The funniest thing was he just appeared to come from nowhere.

When Rasim asked Donald where he met Brooklyn, he didn't say much. Just that he was hanging out front a liquor store one day and dude bought him a bottle and gave him a place to sleep when his parents had the house full of fuck buddies. After that, Rasim and Chance met him, liked him, and they'd been together ever since.

But Brooklyn never, ever, talked about his past. And since the friends didn't like talking about theirs either, the unsaid agreement worked.

Chance, on the other hand, was tall and light skinned with eyes the color of toffee. His mother and father owned a bakery out Maryland and did alright for themselves. They were good parents but since they had him at the age of forty, they were too old to run after him or warn him about life's horrors. Because of it, he had a silent case of Chlamydia and a bout of herpes, which he didn't know about. He assumed he had sunburn on his dick. At least that's what he kept telling his friends.

The teenagers were bopping their heads along with the music but their happiness evaporated when Donald suddenly whipped the car to the curb. At first Rasim assumed he lost what was left of his senses until he saw a cute girl with a pregnant ass switching down the street.

Donald slithered out of the car, whispered in the girl's ear and smacked her so hard she took five steps backwards. To make shit worse, he grabbed her by the forearm and escorted her toward the car.

Rasim's face heated because he wasn't with the abusing women shit. His father taught him to respect the ladies and the elderly and he upheld that belief.

"What the fuck is this nigga doing?" Brooklyn asked as his jaw hung in amazement.

"Do he even know that bitch?" Chance questioned in a high-pitched voice.

"It don't look like it to me," Rasim responded as his eyes blinked as if he were seeing things.

"Man, this nigga 'bout to get us locked up," Brooklyn predicted.

Odd to some, but this was what happened with Donald sometimes and it spooked Rasim out. If he fucked with you, he fucked with you hard and for repayment you would be forced to endure his unpredictable behavior.

The back door flew open and the girl was stuffed inside by way of a shove to the back of her head. She plopped in the seat and her titties smooshed against Brooklyn's lap and her face nestled in the center of Chance's crotch.

As she attempted to get herself together, Donald slammed the door, missing her ankles by mere inches. When she finally repositioned herself in her own seat, she was on Brooklyn's left, next to the window. Without the benefit of an explanation, Donald slid back into the pilot position and eased the car into traffic.

Rasim's heart rate increased as he looked back at the pretty girl with the light brown hair, rosy cheeks and glassy eyes.

Since Donald proceeded as if all was right with the world, although fearful, Rasim could no longer hold his tongue. He wiped his clammy hands on his jeans and asked, "Who dat, man?"

"My personal bitch," he responded flatly, as he eased onto the highway.

Rasim looked back at the girl to check her mental temperature once more. He wasn't sure but something told him that the girl was anything but in a relationship with his friend the lunatic. Maybe it was the rainstorm that rolled down her face or the fact that she was trembling so hard Brooklyn's leg was shaking that gave it away. At any rate, something was off.

"I don't think she want to be here," Rasim said softly. "Maybe you should let her go."

Donald's neck popped in Rasim's direction although his foot was still firmly on the gas pedal and he was pushing sixty miles per hour. "She'll go when I want her to. Now chill out before I lose my patience in this bitch."

Rasim was sitting on the side of the bed looking over at Donald and the girl he practically kidnapped, who he now knew as Sheila. Her entire nature changed. She was giggling like a newborn having its feet tickled, courtesy of the cheap Strawberry MD 20/20 she was quaffing down her throat.

Rasim eyed the entire situation with confusion. *What the fuck was going on?*

One minute she was terrified and the next she couldn't keep her palms off of Donald's dick.

Later, Rasim learned that Donald booked her last week in front of the Shrimp Boat off Benning Road in Southeast Washington, DC. Despite a kiss on his cheek and a promise to stay in contact since he bought her basket of fried shrimp with a large Coke, she failed. So out of revenge, Donald felt warranted in taking her into a semi hostage situation.

Chance and Brooklyn were at the store getting food and would be coming back later. So at the moment Rasim was alone with them.

Suddenly Donald swallowed the rest of the liquor, stood up, gripped Sheila by the forearm and shepherded her toward the bathroom.

When the door was closed Rasim could hear some bumping around before a slight scream rang out on Sheila's part. But the sound was quickly muffled before growing louder again.

Rasim hopped off of the bed and rushed toward the door. He ran his hand from the front to the back of his head as he considered how to approach the matter.

In Rasim's humble opinion, it sounded like the girl was getting raped but he couldn't be sure. He knew his boy could be rough but never heard rape being associated with his brand.

Rasim felt that if he said something wrong, Donald would come thundering out of the bathroom with Rasim in his sights. But, and this was more important, the man in him could not allow what was happening to occur. Not on his watch.

So he not only knocked on the door but he banged on it with authority. Just as he thought, Donald pulled the door open halfway and glared at him. "Be gone, nigga," he said with fire in his eyes. "I'm not in the mood right now." Rasim's eyes trailed from his floating eyeballs down to his dick, which was red and dripping with blood. Donald slammed the door in Rasim's face before he had a chance to hold the memory.

Worried, Rasim dropped to his knees and lowered his head. The dry, gray carpet brushed against his face as he peered through the slat under the door. Now he could see Sheila bent over the toilet throwing up while Donald raped her from behind.

What part of the game is this? Rasim thought.

He leaped up and exploded on the door with heavy fists so hard that his knuckles burned. Through it all Donald did not come out.

Rasim didn't realize until the next morning that he dosed off on the floor from exhaustion. When he finally did, it was far too late.

BY T. STYLES

The cool handcuffs around Rasim's wrists were uncomfortable as he rode in the back of a police car. It had been a long two days since Donald raped Sheila and his life would be changed forever.

For starters, a swift boot to the gut from an angry DC police officer awakened Rasim. Before he could determine what was happening, his arms were seized from the back and he feared his shoulders would pop out of the sockets.

Rasim wasn't alone. His friends Chance and Brooklyn were also arrested and led to the police car as if they all partook in the crime. The only light at the end of the tunnel was that three cars up, he could hear Donald clearly yelling, "Leave my friends alone! They didn't have shit to do with this! I fucked the bitch not them!"

Rasim respected the clarification and he still loved him too. But he wished he hadn't gone so far. He figured it was because of his parents that he was the monster he was.

It wouldn't stop the officers from stuffing the teenagers in their cars and chauffeuring them to the station, only to bombard them with a thousand questions.

In a bitch move, Sheila claimed they all were involved even though her statement couldn't be further from the truth.

The investigation was mental torture on Rasim and his homies. And although spit flew out of the officers' mouths and slapped against their faces as they yelled at Rasim, Brooklyn and Chance, they didn't say a mumbling word.

In the end, Donald would be transported to prison. And Rasim Nami, along with his other homies, were transported to Strawberry Meadows, a group home for troubled youth, thereby breaking his parents' hearts in the process.

BY T. STYLES

CHAPTER 2

SNOW BRADSHAW
WASHINGTON, DC

APRIL 10, 1995

*P*lease don't ask me anything. Please don't ask me anything, Snow chanted repeatedly to herself as she sat across from her parents, Lamont and Maureen Bradshaw, at a huge black lacquer dining room table.

She was awful at mingling and always said the wrong thing.

Her light skin reddened as it did whenever she was in social situations. She felt this way whenever her parents forced her to Nadine's house in the hopes of encouraging Snow to be interested in Nadine's son.

To her right was Morris Hope, a seventeen-year-old church boy with a slight slack jaw problem, which caused his mouth to hang open longer than most. His arm hung around the back of her chair and his sweaty pit brushed against her arm, which made her so annoyed she screamed to the Gods on the inside.

"Dinner is almost ready," Nadine announced as she floated out of the kitchen, wiping her hands on a white hand towel with tiny blue doves spread throughout.

PRISON THRONE

Although she was talking to everyone present, she was observing Snow. Nadine considered her hazel eyes, her naturally light brown skin, and could already see the faces of her grandchildren. In her opinion, Snow could be the answer to her prayers because Morris was as weird as they came and she feared he would never mate.

It was really embarrassing when she went to church with her son—, that the Bradshaw's also attended—only for young women to avoid Morris as if he walked around holding his dick in one hand and a bible in the other.

Girls, who were there to build a relationship with the Lord, would laugh at his hanging jaw often to the point of hysteria.

That was until Nadine spotted Snow.

Yes, precious Snow was the only one at church more gauche than Morris.

"Well, whatever you're cooking it smells delicious," Maureen said as she straightened the collar of her navy blue dress with the huge gold sailor buttons.

When a clump of her graying hair plummeted into her face, Maureen's husband lovingly placed it behind her ear and kissed her on the cheek. Although wrinkles outlined most of the features on her face these days, Lamont still looked upon her with adoration.

Besides, when he ran numbers and sold cocaine on the cold streets of Washington, DC in the '70s, it was Maureen who stood by his side as he attempted to get his shit together. It was Maureen who wrote him letters and visited him in the penitentiary when he needed companionship. And it was Maureen who gave him his first and only child. Snow.

If one were to take a look at the shiny chocolate ball that was Lamont's head and the graying section of hair that dressed its perimeter, they would never see a gangster. But, they would be sadly mistaken.

In his heyday, Lamont was one of the most feared men in DC. Many lost their lives at his hands when they wagered on tic in the numbers, lost and failed to pay. Or took a brick of coke and got ghost. Lamont didn't accept apologies and didn't show mercy either, which was why in his darkest hour, mercy was almost not shown to him.

It was a snowy day when three niggas from New York placed a gun to Lamont's head and stole five kilos of white from the trunk of his money green Mercedes. Of course this enraged the powers that be, despite their history.

His chief, Louie the Knife, had given Lamont his first break into the crime world after he asked for a number and the kid gave him 4578, which netted him fifty thousand dollars.

Under Louie's reign, through the years, Lamont had proven to be smart, vicious and loyal and Louie realized he chose correctly. Lamont always got the money owed, even if it meant taking the lives of the debtors or their family members. He was known on the streets as Lamont of Little Mercy.

But when he was robbed and he couldn't replace the dope or the lucre himself, Louie the Knife had him dragged by his ankles into an abandoned building. Louie loved Lamont, he truly did, but he would treat him like a nigga who raped his granddaughter if he fucked with his cash.

So Louie stood over top of him and was preparing to give the order to drop the fifty-pound cinder block dangling over his face until he yelled, "Please don't, Louie! My wife is pregnant!"

Louie called him a liar until Lamont reminded him how hard he had been hustling to earn money lately. The requests for extra trips to New York while working way past his scheduled time in the process. And the odd jobs for other heavies in the game in search of a larger payday. Suddenly it all made sense to Louie. His dear Lamont was about to become a father.

So Louie the Knife, father of five and grandfather to fifteen, granted him mercy. On two conditions. That he work until he paid off the debt and name his only child after the coke he forfeited. Whether boy or girl, Louie insisted that the child be called Snow.

Lamont never earned a living illegally again.

"Well, I hope everything tastes as good as it smells," Nadine said to Maureen as she played with one of the pearls around her neck. She focused on the children again. "Morris, why don't you take Snow upstairs and show her the script you wrote for the church play next month. I'm sure she'd be interested."

Nadine's suggestion was actually code for, "Get up out of our faces so me and my holy friends can drink a vat of wine as Jesus did."

And as always, the teenagers disappeared upstairs.

The dark closet was awfully tiny and the doorknob stabbing into Snow's coccyx was extremely annoying. Not to mention, she could smell Morris's smelly tennis shoes as he kissed her neck and kneaded her breasts like balls of dough.

BY T. STYLES

It wasn't rape. But it didn't feel good either. He acted this way every time his mother suggested they go upstairs so they could be alone. This activity was one of the reasons she despised visiting.

As his slippery tongue ran along the side of her neck and dipped into her ear canal, she wanted to scream. His spit clogged up her ear and made it hard to hear on the left side.

Snow hated how he felt against her body. Against her skin. Most of all, she hated how his stiff penis poked at her belly as he accosted her with promises to fuck her so well.

She wasn't worried about things going too far in the sexual department though. Both of them were virgins and neither was brave enough to go against God's will. They just chose to shame him instead by humping in the darkness, hoping he couldn't see their filthy ways.

"Your titties feel so good," Morris said breathing heavily against her clavicle. "I'm gonna fuck you so well."

"Okay," she said, being a teenager of few words.

"You like how it feels, Snow? You want me to fuck you so well?"

"Yes."

He gripped both of her large breasts at the same time and squeezed as if he were preparing to pop huge pimples. "You gonna be my wife, Snow. Wait, you'll see. We will be together for the rest of our lives."

Stop the fucking presses!

Hearing that madness caused her heart to tap in her chest and pump into overdrive. She thought about the three days a week she went to church with her parents that didn't include Sunday. She thought about Morris's weird way of squeezing her that caused her stomach to swirl. Most of all, she thought about his hanging jaw that even at the moment

PRISON THRONE

rubbed against her clavicle and tickled. She did not want this for her life. She did not want any of it.

So she shoved him into his hanging clothes and walked out of the closet. Considering how grossed out she was, it was probably appropriate to run but everything Snow did was dry. She was so boring that even in the dramatic situation, she moved at a snail's pace down the stairs.

When she made it to the bottom, she stopped. From where she stood, she saw her parents swallowing crystal glasses of red wine as they chuckled like beefy sailors at sea.

A vat of Merlot, almost empty, sat next to them.

Stupid mothafuckas, she thought.

If only she were brave enough to say it out loud.

She was still staring at them until Lamont turned his head, looked at Snow and covered his mouth. Immediately he rushed toward her as if she were an open quarterback with the ball on a football field.

When he was upon her, he slammed down her shirt and glared.

In her haste, Snow had forgotten to adjust her clothing after leaving the closet and her daddy had seen it all. Before the correction, her shirt and bra sat on the top of her breasts, which forced her boobies downward and to swing like pendulums on a clock.

Things were a blur for Snow after that moment. The embarrassment she felt was so heavy that although she could hear her parents' muffled voices, she didn't understand a word they were saying.

She witnessed Maureen grab the keys from the dining room table and yank her purse off of the chair's arm.

BY T. STYLES

That quickly, Snow was ushered out of the house by her father and pushed into the car. Despite it being the most embarrassing experience of her life, Snow was too boring to shed a tear.

Snow sat at a much smaller dining room table in her parents' house and ate dry rice, no salt or butter. Unlike Nadine, who dabbled in the real estate industry, her parents were telephone operators and earned a meager pay.

Maureen wasn't much of a cook so Snow was certain that the soggy fried chicken on her plate would be bloody red in the center. The most tragic part of the evening was that because Snow's titties hung low at Nadine's house, they weren't able to have a decent meal.

After Lamont forced his food down and begged his body not to regurgitate it and hurt his wife's feelings in the process, he focused on Snow. "Honey, what did he do to you?"

Snow raised her eyes from her plate and focused on her father. She loved him. She loved both of her parents but she wasn't happy and she didn't know why.

Not only that, but Snow didn't want to talk about the situation. It was embarrassing enough as is. She preferred to fade into the walls but neither would give her the honor.

With her upper body slouched over, for the hundredth time, she said, "He didn't do anything to me, daddy."

"Then why were you undressed?" Maureen asked in a soft voice. She cared about Snow so much that it was etched all over her face. Her bottom lip trembled and it was clear she expected the worst. Rape.

"Because he was touching me." She shrugged. "That's all."

Although relieved, Lamont didn't like the idea one bit. He didn't care if the kids stole a kiss or two before the age of eighteen but grabbing nipples and shit was out of the question! "Did he make you, you know..."

"No," she huffed.

"Did he hurt you?" Maureen asked.

"I said no, mama."

"Then what is going on?" Lamont roared.

"I'm bored with life," Snow admitted. "Terribly!" she yelled. It was as if she had reached an orgasm because it was the first time she used her angry voice.

Lamont and Nadine were shocked. They leaned back in their chairs and allowed their chins to swing just...like...Morris's.

"I don't get it," Lamont screamed, trying to regain control of his family. "How could you possibly be bored? We're at church every other day. You have friends who you visit and with God in your life, it's always a great day."

"Praise be to God," Maureen added waving both hands in the air.

He sounded so fucking stupid.

So did she.

The friends he spoke of didn't exist because even if she did hang with the girls, they always ignored her and treated her like an outcast.

Snow's head tilted as she tried to understand how any of what he said sounded exciting. But instead of answering she asked, "May I please be excused?"

"Yes, honey, but hurry back," Maureen responded. "We have a lot to talk about."

Snow scooted back in her seat and the chair's legs made a screeching noise against the hardwood floors. She strolled toward the stairwell, which was out of her parents' view, and crept into the basement.

In her earlier years, she danced down there but she no longer possessed the verve to move her limbs. Sadly, twirling had exited her heart long ago.

She ambled past the large mirrors on the wall and toward a huge wooden chest that sat on the floor with a hanging combination padlock attached.

Knowing the code was 4578—the number Lamont gave Louie the Knife—because he told the story a million times, she gained access. The lock popped open and with a soft tug she grabbed what she wanted from inside.

She slogged up the stairs toward the front door, clasped her father's keys and walked out of the house without informing her parents.

Once inside of her father's navy blue 1994 Honda Prelude, she drove a mile up the street to the 7-Eleven. Parking the car in two spots at the same time, she grabbed the item from her father's chest, walked into the store and pointed the gun at the store's employee.

"Hands in the air," she said so dryly the cashier giggled. "This is a stickup."

With her work done, Snow walked into the house, leaving the gun and the money she'd stolen on the driver's seat of the car. When she bent the corner to the dining room, her parents were still at the table...waiting.

"What took you so long?" Lamont asked with a lowered brow. "Is your stomach upset?"

This bitch better not be pregnant, he thought.

"No. I'm fine."

"Well what's up, baby?" Maureen asked, only five seconds away from crying. "You're scaring me."

Before she could respond, the front of their house lit up in an amazing display of red and blue lights. The thundering sound of police banging on the door startled everyone but Snow.

There was no use in Snow leaving the table. If they wanted her, they would have their way and there wasn't a thing she could do about it. Instead, she remained calm, grabbed the cold undercooked chicken, took a bite and waited for her new fate.

Snow sat in the van and glanced out of the window as it drove down the street. A few other girls were inside and although they introduced themselves to one another, nobody bothered to speak to her. She didn't care much; at least that's what her mind said. Besides, she'd had a long week and all she wanted to do was be alone.

After robbing the store, she was evaluated by a psychiatrist because it was totally unlike Snow. She was a straight 'A' student and every member in the church's congregation spoke in her defense. It was agreed that for whatever reason, she simply snapped. However, she still needed to be punished.

BY T. STYLES

So Snow was remanded to Strawberry Meadows Group Home. In her parents' honest opinion, after Slack Jaw Morris placed his hands on her she probably lost reason, and when the judge saw the spit juice collecting in the corners of his mouth, she agreed.

When the bus stopped in front of a building that resembled anything but a home, Snow's body trembled. It wasn't until then that she realized that all of her life she had the benefit of her parents' love and protection. But who would protect her now?

Strawberry Meadows was a co-ed facility for children who were not totally bad, but on the verge of getting into trouble. Although the program was meant to put troubled teenagers back on track, they didn't have enough employees to handle the one hundred and twenty kids who roamed the halls. As a result, it was a breeding ground for strife.

"Get off the bus!" yelled a white woman who hopped on the vehicle when the doors opened. She was a mammoth sized beast with huge eyes and boulders for fists. "You're at Strawberry Meadows now! In here, I'm your mama!" Although she preferred the *mother* moniker, the children called her Ms. Brush Face behind her back. She had so much hair on her face you could barely see her eyes.

Snow popped up from her seat and entered the line of girls moving toward the exit. Tears rolled down her cheeks as she made her way toward the entrance.

She would hate it there!

She was sure of it!

Until she walked through the doors and saw Rasim.

Now everything she went through made sense.

God had brought her there to meet him.

PRISON THRONE

CHAPTER 3

RASIM

Rasim, Chance and Brooklyn illegally occupied the room of ten girls. Basically, they were going through their personal shit. Unfortunately, all of the girls were at a Wellness Seminar meant to advise them on protected sex and STDs and the friends took full advantage of their absence.

The boys were not even supposed to be in the Girls' Wing. Their hall was on the opposite end of the building. But Rasim and his friends did everything but follow the rules.

Brooklyn sat on a bottom bunk examining the insides of a red duffle bag. "Look at this shit," he yelled holding a rubber dick in the air. "This bitch horny as shit." He tossed it to the floor and proceeded to pilfer. He was low-key mad that women had a toy to satisfy their needs. Where was his portable pussy?

"Who is that again?" Chance asked with sly eyes while looking down at the rubber ding-dong. Why trouble with a fake when he held the real thing? So he wanted her name so that he could attempt to dick her down later. He was standing in front of the bed going through a ripped black suitcase on the top bunk. The clinic cured him of Chlamydia and now he was ready to use his new stick.

"The bitch with the big nose and sores around her mouth," Brooklyn advised, pointing at his own nostrils.

"You don't want that." He shook his head in disgust. "Trust me."

He could speak for himself. Chance pulled up her face in his mental Rolodex and was determined to have his stick in her mouth before the night's end.

"You better get that shit checked out first," Rasim said going through a blue suitcase across the room. "I saw you scratching your joint earlier today."

"Fuck you looking at my dick for?" Chance laughed.

"Nigga, you was standing next to me while I was killing mothafuckas in Spades. You don't remember that shit?"

"You better watch that nigga reference," Brooklyn joked while pointing at him. "We can protect you when you're with us but you could get your shit cracked if you dolo." He focused back on the bag. "Remember, youngin', you brown, not black."

"It's the same thing," Chance interrupted as he picked up another bag. The other didn't yield any benefits. "If you ain't white, you fall in the same category. Nigga."

While they joked on one another, Rasim went into his heart. It troubled him that his heritage was often the topic of discussion. Truthfully, although he was Pakistani, he was often confused with Indian or Hawaiian people. His features could be mistaken for any number of races.

Eventually Rasim brushed the shit off his shoulders when he found five dollars in a bag. He tucked it in his pocket and moved to the next duffle when Brooklyn yelled, "Ain't these old ass mothafuckas the parents of the girl who came today?" He was clutching a picture of Lamont and Maureen Bradshaw in his paws. A baby blue duffle bag belonging to Snow sat at his feet.

Snow's parents rode up to the center after she was registered.

Rasim stared at the picture and said, "Yeah, that's them." He returned his focus to the bag he was robbing. Besides, the girl was cute, really cute, but she didn't talk. She roamed around like a mummy and it crept him out.

"You better watch that chick," Brooklyn quipped as he eyed Rasim. "She be staring at you like she gonna eat you alive. She may be a cannibal and shit."

"Who you talking about?" Chance questioned. "Church girl?"

"Yep."

Chance nodded when he recalled her hazel eyes, big breasts and pretty face. "I'm telling you now, if you don't hit that I will. Flat butt and all. That's on my mother's heart."

The three of them laughed because it was true. Snow was a looker. The only thing that messed Snow up in her own opinion was that although she had a pretty face and huge titties, her buttocks were as flat as Monday's newspaper.

"Yeah, she lacking in that area for sure," Rasim admitted. "God must've put too much up top and didn't have nothing left for the bottom. But leave that girl alone, Chance. She seems nice."

Brooklyn and Chance paused before both of them erupted into laughter. They performed as if they were in their own room and could make as much noise as they wanted.

"You feeling Pancakes, huh?" Brooklyn joked.

"I'm not saying that," he frowned. "All I'm saying is that she 'aight and to leave her alone. You mothafuckas always go too far and shit."

"Okay, but if you want to fuck her just remember she's wearing these," Brooklyn said raising a pair of big panties.

Rasim walked over to him, grabbed the yellow bloomers and swung them around. Thinking the shit was hysterical, Brooklyn and Chance did the same thing by grabbing other pairs. They resembled Jamaicans at a party waving flags in the air.

They were in full fool mode when Snow entered and paused at the doorway. When she saw them laughing at her expense with her drawers in their hands, her heart dropped to her belly. She couldn't believe the sight and the embarrassment caused her face to itch.

Trying to understand what she'd done so wrong, her eyes rolled over Brooklyn and her things that sat on the floor. When she considered him long enough, she observed Chance whose eyes were as wide as the gateway to hell. But when she looked at Rasim, she was devastated. The disappointed mien she wore let Rasim know how deeply he hurt her feelings. And it fucked with him too.

In a panic, she dodged out of the room, crying the whole way.

⚜⚜ ⚜⚜
🝖 🝖

Rasim looked all over Strawberry Meadows before he finally found Snow sitting in the Movie Room. It was the place the staff played VHS tapes on the weekends for those who didn't have passes to go home. Or families to go home to.

PRISON THRONE

Snow was sitting on the sofa with her thighs pressed against her body. Her forehead rested on her knees as she sobbed quietly.

Since the radio was playing, Rasim figured she turned it on to conceal her weeping.

As he stood over top of her, he struggled with what to say. He didn't even know the chick and had no idea why he was so concerned. But he moved closer anyway and sat next to her.

At first Snow thought the person sitting down was just another boy who had taken an interest in her. She raised her head and was surprised that it was Rasim instead, seeing as how he was so damn mean. Still, she scooted away from him, closer to the arm of the couch. Taking a moment to wipe her tears with the ball of tissue clutched in her hand, she rested her head back on her knees.

"You 'aight?" Rasim asked looking over at her.

She nodded on her knees.

"Then why you crying?"

She shrugged.

Damn! Why she gotta be so fucking weird? He thought.

"Look, I'm sorry about that shit in your room just now. I didn't mean to hurt your feelings and stuff."

Finally, she looked directly into his eyes. At that moment, Rasim thought he was looking at another chick because he had never been so close to her face before. His heart rate sped up as he examined her features. Her skin was fair and she was saucer-eyed, allowing him to see the hazel hue of her irises. She was more beautiful up close and Rasim was gone.

BY T. STYLES

Suddenly his tongue fluttered around in his mouth as he boxed with what to say next. "I…I didn't mean to get you upset."

She wiped her tears with the sleeve of her t-shirt. "Then why did you?"

Wow! Even her voice is pretty, he thought. *She should use it more.*

Her tone was breathy like Marilyn Monroe's and he hadn't expected her to talk that way.

Rasim knew he had to compose himself before he looked like a fool so he said, "I was just fucking around with my friends. I didn't mean nothing by it. Really."

She looked away from him and he was relieved. Now he could check his red Polo shirt and blue jeans to make sure he was still fresh.

Just then "You're All That I Need" by Method Man and Mary J. Blige came on the radio and he watched her move her lips although no sound came out. It was clear that it was her favorite song.

"I'm fine," she said out of the blue. She looked at him again and he swallowed. "Thank you for asking." She rubbed her arms because it was chilly in the room.

"If you fine, why you still crying?" he questioned.

She sighed and looked down at her legs. "Because all my life people have ignored me. Made fun of me. Just because I have a flat butt and I'm not as cute as other girls. And I guess…well, I guess I thought when I got here people would treat me differently. I'm tired of being alone."

Rasim shook his head. He understood how it felt to be an outcast because although he had friends, he was always judged for his religion and ethnicity. "I get that," he nodded.

PRISON THRONE

When she rubbed her arms again she asked, "Is it cold in here or is it just me?"

"Yes," he admitted. It was definitely chilly. He felt that the staff was trying to freeze niggas out and shit.

When he saw her shivering, Rasim reached into his pocket and pulled out a pair of her underwear and placed them over her right shoulder. "Maybe these are big enough to keep you warm."

At first she was horrified, believing he was doing an outstanding job of insulting her, until he flashed the smile that made him young boy famous.

Suddenly giggling felt good. Like butterflies tickling the inside of her stomach but better. It wasn't until that moment that she realized she had never really laughed.

"You see," he said running his finger along the side of her face. Now that he had his swag back, he would use it to the fullest. "Make time to laugh at the dumb shit. Besides, even with that flat butt, with a face like yours, you still a ten."

Rasim squeezed her cheek lightly, stood up and bopped out.

In Snow's personal opinion, Rasim was the grooviest nigga ever!

CHAPTER 4

RASIM

A few days later, the small cafeteria was heavy with juvenile delinquents. Rasim, Brooklyn and Chance just finished stacking their plates as high as they could without them smacking against the floor. On their fat boy shit, they made their way to their favorite table.

Many girls eyed them as they moved because they were the cutest guys in the group home. It wasn't a crew of niggas who even came close. They were winning.

And Snow definitely agreed.

Rasim placed his tray on the table and Brooklyn sat on his left while Chance perched on the right.

The moment Rasim was comfortable he realized he forgot his silverware. "Damn," he said wanting to dive into the spaghetti that Mrs. Corner made. He loved when she was in the kitchen because her food was always seasoned to perfection. He considered using his fingers he was so hungry. "I left my fucking fork."

He was about to get up and get one when Snow, with a lowered head, placed a fork and napkin on his table and slouched away.

Rasim turned around and looked at the pretty girl who hadn't said a word to him since the movie room as she made her way back to her own plate.

"Man, that girl is too fucking weird," Brooklyn whispered, shaking his head. "How the fuck she know you needed that shit? Too creepy for me."

"I don't know, Rasim," Chance responded while shoving his fork in his face. "She looks like she stalking, young. Betta watch that bitch."

While they maintained their own perspectives, Rasim felt differently. Lately things had been done for him that he didn't ask for and he was grateful.

Never taking care of himself a day in his life, he would do stuff like wash his clothes and leave them wet in the machine. When he finally remembered, after having zero boxers of course, they would be dried, folded and sitting on his bed.

Snow didn't stop there. If he rubbed his temples due to the headaches he often got in class, he would go to break and return to two Tylenol sitting on his desk with a cup of water.

Snow wanted to take care of him because she was good at it and he was falling for her. *Hard.*

She became even more interesting when he learned what the young girl was in Strawberry Meadows for. At first he figured she was fucking up in school or playing hooky to earn a stint in the home. Imagine his surprise when he discovered the baby goon was arrested for holding up a 7-Eleven.

No doubt Snow had more heart than any nigga in the Meadows. And that went for Brooklyn and Chance too.

It was Sunday morning and Rasim stood in the rec room playing Pac Man on a video machine. From the corner of his eye he watched everyone, including Brooklyn and Chance, make their way to the chapel to worship.

Although Brooklyn went to ask God to forgive the things he had already done and the things he had written down for the future, Chance participated because he derived that the fattest butt girls were always present. He even tested his theory by counting them as they walked the line one Sunday.

Rasim's homies went to the service for Christians but there was a Muslim ritual being conducted at the same time in another location. There were at least five children of Muslim faith who invited Rasim but he always refused. He didn't want his friends seeing him praising Allah when he wanted to be like them.

Snow walked toward the chapel with her black leather Bible clutched against her breasts. Not wanting to bother Rasim, she was preparing to hustle past him when he stepped away from the machine and blocked her.

Snow was 5'7", which some considered tall for a girl, but standing in front of Rasim she felt like a dwarf. "What's up with you?" he asked.

She shrugged.

"How come you do stuff for me but never say shit?"

She shrugged twice for good measure.

He placed his hands on her forearms and squeezed lightly. "Snow, say my name," he rocked her softly.

"Rasim," she said in a tone that got his dick hard. She looked over at the video machine and then up into his eyes again. "You aren't going to worship today?"

Luckily for Snow, she uttered the magic words that caused him to release her as he made his way back over to the machine. "I don't have to worship." He slipped a quarter in the slot. "I already know there's a God."

She frowned. "Then come with me and prove it."

"That's not my thing, Snow. Everybody got their own thing."

She shook her head sadly. "You shouldn't turn your back on God, Rasim. You never know when you might need Him."

⚜ ⚜

Rasim sat in the rec room playing cards with Queen who had wanted him from day one. She was as awful in Spades as a pitbull puppy in a room full of new Jordans. But he didn't have another partner because when it came to Spades, Brooklyn and Chance acted as if they were newlyweds who didn't want to cheat on each other.

When Rasim stared out in frustration, he saw Snow sitting in front of the TV. Every now and again she would look at him but then focus back on the show. He knew what she was doing—determining how else she could serve him—and she had a nigga feeling like a king. Dudes were salty when it came to the attention the cute red bone had blessed Rasim with and it showed in their glares.

She was the weirdest chick he ever came in contact with in his life and he never met anyone like her. That made her more than special. It made her unique.

When Rasim found out that Queen threw out a high Spade to cut his high Spade when she held a lower card in her hand, he grew frustrated. "Damn, girl. Why you didn't throw out a lower Spade the last hand? You cut your own partner and shit. I thought all you was holding was high cards."

"Leave her alone," Chance laughed.

"Yeah, ya'll not losing by that much anyway," Brooklyn added.

Rasim's nostrils flared and he said, "Get up, Queen. You cut."

"I'm cut?" she repeated with an attitude. "How you figure?"

"Because you can't play, now bounce."

Queen scooted from the table during one of Snow's head turns when she was checking to see if Rasim needed anything. So he waved her over and she came hither.

Several male teenagers wanted to steal Rasim in his jaw they were so fucking jealous. The problem was that although Rasim was not a gangster, Brooklyn and Chance could not say the same.

When Snow was standing across from him in front of Queen's chair he said, "Sit down."

Snow took Queen's seat without a word and Brooklyn and Chance eyed the couple.

"You know how to play Spades?"

"I do alright," she said softly.

"Then prove it."

And it was so.

Game after game, Rasim and Snow beat the brakes off of Brooklyn and Chance and their winning streak was no more. It was so bad that other teenagers gathered to see Rasim and Snow rule.

Snow appeared to come alive as she slammed her cards down on the table with authority, resulting in stolen book after stolen book.

PRISON THRONE

After her Spades swag was displayed, if he didn't know it before, he knew it then. That pretty bitch was made especially for him.

It was midnight and all of the teenagers were supposed to be in bed. But as usual, Rasim and his friends didn't respect authority.

The odor of detergent was overpowering as Rasim pressed Queen against the wall in the dark laundry room. He kissed her deeply while he fingered her pussy so long his digit stiffened.

Rasim was somewhat impressed. She didn't know how to play Spades but her pussy was clean and he appreciated that. The saddest part of it all was that although Queen was willing, Rasim didn't want to be there. His mind was on Snow and he wondered where her head was. If she was thinking of him.

Queen was okay. He discovered she had aspirations and he respected that. She dreamed of being a boss and declared that she would have her own business someday. She was cool if sluts were what you were in to.

In addition to her brains, she was aggressive. She yanked Rasim by his collar after their conversation for a little more intimacy earlier in the day. Although he wanted Snow, she moved too slowly after the game was over. She basically retreated, giving Queen full clemency. Big mistake.

Across the way, Brooklyn had Nicky on top of the washing machine as he suckled her breasts. And there was no way Rasim and Brooklyn would be doing their thing without Chance getting in on the fun too. True to his word he was standing in the corner getting his diseased dickey sucked by Big Angie, the girl with the duffle bag dildo.

Although he freaked Queen, Rasim's mind floated once again to Snow. He thought about how after they won a total of six matches, Snow bought Rasim a soda because she overheard him telling Brooklyn that he was thirsty. But after the deed, like she had in the past, she dipped off.

Ironically, a strange thing was happening between Rasim and Snow. The more space she provided him, the more he wanted to be around her. He was used to women pressing him out for his time and attention.

Queen stripped her lips away from Rasim and whispered, "I like you, Rasim. A lot."

"I like you too," he responded, kissing her neck.

"You and your friends are so cool."

"Of course," he whispered kissing her chin. "You're dealing with a king amongst kings."

She giggled. "Come on, Ras. Fuck me." She was getting hornier with each flip of her clit and was willing to go the extra mile. Especially since Chance and Brooklyn had their strumpets with their hands on the dryers as they pounded them from the back.

Within seconds, the smell of detergent was washed away and replaced with the scent of young girls who didn't know how to wash their pussies properly. The odor teetered the line between a couple bushels of crabs and a block of brie cheese.

Rasim couldn't see the girl's face but he could feel her passion. "We can do that later," he said as he moved in for another kiss and started playing with her box that, quite frankly, was getting a little dry.

Queen wasn't about the foreplay shit. Straight up, she wanted to fuck.

"Rasim, stop playing," she whispered in his face. "I know you got a condom."

"I don't."

"Go get one from Brooklyn then. I heard him tell Nicky that he had a whole bag under his bunk."

Rasim exhaled and said, "Aight. I'll be back."

When he left he thought about what Queen wanted to do. The way she threw her kitty around the group home had him concerned about feeding the cat. Not only that but after awhile the laundry room smelled like Trash Pussy Soup.

But, there was something else on his mind too.

Away from Queen, Rasim crept into his room that was full of sleeping boys and brushed his teeth. He didn't like the way she tasted in his mouth. It wasn't nasty. It just wasn't right. Instead of looking for condoms, he tiptoed down the dark hallway toward Snow's room.

When he made it to her dorm's door, he walked past it once and then again. He knew he couldn't knock because nine other girls shared the room with her, minus the one who was getting banged out in the laundry room by Chance.

Feeling stupid, he was about to turn around when Snow opened the door, walked out into the hallway and leaned up against the wall. She looked down at the floor with her arms crossed over her chest. Unlike Queen with her tight fitting clothing, Snow was wearing baggy gray sweats, her favorite attire.

How did she know he was there?

Her stance resembled a child who was bored and desired to play and it made Rasim want to protect her. He never felt that way about anyone in his young life.

Instead of saying anything to her, he decided to play the mute game with Snow. He grabbed her by the hand and led her to another room in the group home. The fact that Ms. Brush Face could come out at any time and deport his ass out of the facility excited Rasim even more.

When they made it to the small, dark conference room that was used for lawyer visits, Rasim pushed a table in front of the door. It wouldn't stop Ms. Brush Face from breaking the bitch down if she was so inclined but it would buy him a few seconds.

With his barrier in place, he turned around and looked at Snow. There was just enough luminosity streaming in through the windows across the way due to the lights outside of the property. Slowly he walked toward her and gazed into her sparkling hazel eyes.

He was fully expecting her to remain silent as usual but instead she whispered, "I love you."

Rasim was blown away.

Snow didn't speak much but when she did she spoke levels.

"I know," he responded.

Forever socially awkward, she asked, "Can I do anything for you?"

He smiled. "I don't want you to do anything you don't want."

"I think you're perfect," she admitted looking down at the floor again. "In my eyes, you're Superman." This time she stared into his eyes.

Rasim's heart beat wildly. Damn, this chick was for him. He was too young to feel like a grown ass man, yet

Snow did that for him. "What did I do to earn a tag like that, Snow?"

"Whenever I'm around you, you make me feel stronger," she whispered.

That was it.

Rasim was done.

He lowered his head and kissed her gently on the lips. With their mouths connected, they eased down to the dirty brown carpet. Snow was on her back and Rasim was careful not to apply too much pressure. He could feel Snow's body warming up and he was rock hard.

Since Rasim had brushed his teeth moments earlier, the minty flavor of his lips had Snow tickled wet. It was a far cry from Morris's swinging jaw, that was for sure. Snow found herself wanting to go to the next level, which was something she'd never done before. Emboldened, she stripped her lips from his and stared into his eyes. She swallowed and said, "I'm ready, Rasim. You can have sex with me if you want. I give my life to you."

Now it was Rasim who would take a few moments to gulp some air because he held a secret not even his friends knew about. "Snow, I never...like...you know."

If he was talking to another girl, she would know exactly what he meant but Snow simply wasn't the type. The strict routine she grew up around succeeded in stealing any creativity from her mind so she was always confused. If Rasim wanted to explain something to Snow, he had better come out and say it.

"I don't understand," she whispered.

Rasim sat up and leaned against the wall. Snow crawled in the same direction and sat next to him before allowing her head to rest against his shoulder. Both of them looked toward the window and Rasim played with his fingers. What he was prepared to share with Snow he'd never revealed. "I never been with a girl before," he mumbled. "Sexually."

Oh.

Now Snow was hip.

"I never been with a girl either," she responded seriously.

Rasim busted out laughing but Snow didn't find the humor. She didn't make jokes and she wasn't making one then. That was something else he liked about her. She was robotic, beautiful and innocent at the same time.

How she do that? He thought.

"I hope not," he chuckled. At first, the fact that he didn't have sex made him feel inadequate. But around Snow, all was well in the world.

She raised her head and looked over at him. "Do you want to have sex with me now? Because I want to have sex with you."

"But what if I hurt you?"

"At least I'll know I'm alive."

Once again, Snow amazed him with her word play and they found their way back to the floor. Rasim removed her sweatpants first, followed by the big yellow panties he waved in the air. It was somewhat poetic that she had them joints on.

Naked from the waist down, slowly and carefully Rasim entered her tightness. Rasim was heavily endowed so he would stop whenever Snow bit down on her bottom lip to check for pressure. He wasn't trying to hurt her. He wasn't even trying to cum. All he wanted was to share this experience with someone he cared about, and someone who cared about him.

But, just like any good sex act, after awhile it got good for the both of them. Rasim felt the fine hairs over his body rise and his lower belly heat up.

Oh the feeling!

Pure bliss!

Even Snow, who never had an orgasm in her weird life, began to tremble. At least Rasim had the benefit of a dick jerk or two but this was Snow's first. Her toes spread in her tennis and she convulsed as a tingling sensation with electric shock power coursed through her body. In the end, she was successful. She had reached an orgasm and Rasim was her first.

He was right behind her as he lowered his head and kissed her softly. Although he wanted to be nastier, he figured the first time should be special as he exploded his semen into her body. He moaned far louder than Snow, that's for sure, as he was drained.

Something happened that neither one of them could deny.

Rasim and Snow had officially fallen in love.

BY T. STYLES

CHAPTER 5

SNOW

S now stood in front of the mirror in the small dance room within the group home. Dressed in black tights and a red top, she hit play on the radio and Boyz II Men's hit song "On Bended Knee" blasted from the speakers.

Before moving, she observed her reflection, and the body she had grown to hate. Her jaw was too squared. Her eyes were too light and her butt had zero curves. In no way was she attractive or sexy for that matter, to hear her tell it. She was an ugly monster who should've stayed with Slack Jaw Morris, gotten married and lived a miserable life.

But when she closed her eyes and listened to the words of the song and thought about Rasim and what they shared last night, something compelling occurred. She stopped coming down so hard on herself and felt powerful. She felt elevated and her body swayed to the moving notes.

Snow's eyes remained closed as she rocked back and forth. Her arms became wings and she was free to fly.

The music pushed into her chest. Into her heart and forced her to cry. She denied her art for far too long and she was consumed with guilt, which made the performance all the more special.

An older dancer once told her that the only sin greater than suicide was denying a God given talent and she would never allow that to happen again.

When the song was over she opened her eyes, looked at her reflection in the mirror and smiled.

She was back and she had Rasim to thank.

The aroma of Pine Sol was powerful as Snow and Mute Candy cleaned the tables. Each person had one chore but Snow greedily requested two. As a result, she was in charge of decontaminating the cafeteria as well as the bathrooms. Using her hands prevented her mind from wandering so she appreciated the extra tasks.

To say she did a good job was an understatement. Snow got into her chores so well that one kid dropped his pizza on the bathroom floor on the cheese side. He wasn't concerned. He just picked it up and ate it anyway. After all, Snow cleaned the fuck out of that floor.

Basically, she had two jobs at Strawberry Meadows, cleaning and caring for Rasim, and she did both with pride. Rasim's side of the room was so immaculate that Southeast Brian and a few of his boys took to telling Ms. Brush Face that Snow was doing his chores in the hopes of stunting his groove. They were in for a surprise when each received a solid tongue lashing for smelling like weed and were thrown into a two-week suspension.

After Snow was sure the cafeteria and bathrooms were unblemished, she sat on the couch in the recreation room and pulled her legs to her body. It was her most comfortable position.

Since Rasim left Strawberry Meadows on a visit with his family, she was alone and bored. If she wasn't with him, she was thinking about him and she liked it that way.

BY T. STYLES

It gave her something to look forward to because although he didn't say he loved her, Rasim made it clear that he cared.

In her spare time, mostly on the days Rasim was not around, she danced. She danced so much that her ankles throbbed but it felt terrific.

In the mood for music, Snow turned the radio on just as Mute Candy walked inside.

Mute Candy was a cute girl with chocolate skin and long, fine, black hair that ran down her back. Some thought she was Indian but she was one hundred percent African American.

If it were true that Snow was Queen Awkward, then Mute Candy was the Princess. Born speechless, Mute Candy never said a mumbling word. Her mother, Diane Dallas, loved Candy as hard as any mother could and sometimes it showed. If only she could've kicked her crack habit, all would've been well in Candy's world. Instead, throughout school she was picked on, abused and laughed at until recently.

One day a predator decided that since Mute Candy couldn't talk she probably couldn't defend herself either. He decided to push her into a pile of overgrown grass behind her high school in an attempt to rape her. Bad move. But how was he to know that Candy kept a switchblade on her person at all times?

The child couldn't talk!

Mute Candy activated the knife so quickly that the blade flew open and clicked. She wasted no second plunging it into the flesh of his stomach and when he tried to crawl away she jabbed his spine too. Blood spurted on everything she wore but she was unfazed as she evolved from victim to predator. Before long, he was paralyzed.

PRISON THRONE

When her work was done she looked down at him and felt it was good but it was time to get a little creative. Mute Candy pushed whatever she could find on the ground into his mouth to prevent him from making a sound. When he was stuffed like a Thanksgiving turkey, she stuck him again.

This is where it gets weird.

Every day for three days, Mute Candy would walk back to the same brush and stick the rapist at least five times in his thighs. Mice would chew on his flesh at night and she loved it. At one point she busted him in the head with a glass bottle, but that was for free.

When she came back on the fourth day the rapist was gone. An old woman looking for cans saw him and called 911 for help, after she searched his pockets for money of course.

When the rapist was in the hospital he had the nerve to tell the authorities that Mute Candy assaulted him without warrant. In a twist of events, mainly because Mute Candy never mentioned that she was almost sexually assaulted, she was thrown in Strawberry Meadows and he was set free. Things could've been far worse had it not been for the man having a record as a sexual pervert so for that, Mute Candy was grateful.

Sitting next to Snow, Mute Candy grabbed a box of Uno cards and started dealing Snow and herself a hand. She didn't even ask if Snow wanted to play. She was just like Snow actually, able to express herself without words.

Snow looked at Mute Candy, smiled and proceeded to throw out a yellow four.

And that's how Mute Candy and Snow became best friends.

BY T. STYLES

It wasn't until that moment that Snow realized that she didn't come to Strawberry Meadows just for Rasim. She came for Mute Candy too.

After playing cards with Mute Candy and talking to her via pencil and paper, Snow decided to go to the library and locate a book on sign language. If Mute Candy was going to be her very good best girlfriend, she wanted to be able to talk to her without pencil and paper.

When she found the book of her choice, she strolled toward her room and saw a picture lying on her bed. It was of her in the dance room on the day she was wearing the black tights and a red shirt.

Who took it?

Her jaw dangled as she eyed each detail of the picture. Someone managed to capture how she felt when she was dancing and she looked like a goddess.

Her right arm reached into the heavens and her fingers curved ever so lightly. Her left arm extended toward the right and she was on the tips of her toes.

And then there was the silhouette of her body that was simply breathtaking. It was as if Michelangelo returned to earth just to assist the photographer with taking the perfect picture.

On the back of the photo it read, *"If I'm Superman, you're Mona Lisa. Love, Rasim."*

Just as she thought.

Rasim was perfect.

And Snow cried tears of joy.

At first Snow was cleaning the bathroom but now she was doubled over the toilet vomiting. She couldn't understand why she was so sick and she was about to call her mother until Ms. Brush Face walked in and discovered her.

Looking down at the ill child, she placed her hands on her hips and shook her head. "Not you too."

"What do you mean?" Snow whispered.

"Come with me," she replied with a shake of her head.

Snow did the best she could to get herself together. She followed Ms. Brush Face toward a small office, the entire time wondering what she'd done wrong.

Ms. Brush Face plopped down while Snow stood in front of her desk awaiting her next orders.

"Piss in this," Ms. Brush Face said handing her a plastic cup. "The bathroom is over there."

Like a robot, Snow walked toward the bathroom, pulled her clothes down, squatted and pissed in the cup over the toilet. When she was done, she cleaned the outside really well, dried it off and handed it back to Ms. Brush Face.

Ms. Brush Face dipped a stick into the urine, causing it to splash on her knuckles but she didn't give a fuck. She waited a few seconds and read the results.

Shaking her head, she said, "You're pregnant. Your parents are going to be devastated."

Upon hearing the worst news of her life, Snow Bradshaw passed out cold.

CHAPTER 6

RASIM

R asim, Brooklyn and Chance were in their room talking about the recent trip home Rasim was granted. This one was for the books.

It had been a little over a month since the first time he had sex with Snow and it had been happening repeatedly ever since. But now that Rasim had his first experience, he took to flinging his dick around like he was a kid and it was a brand new sword.

His latest conquest?

Selena Amo.

While it was true that sex with Snow was as special as hugging a newborn baby, simply put, the pretty Latina knew how to fuck. Selena sucked, licked, scratched and sexed Rasim into oblivion the entire weekend he was home on a pass. And just like young teenage boys do, he thought it would be a good idea to brag. Besides, all three of them had their way with Selena and they needed to compare notes.

Even though conversations about fucking Selena were free, he never said a word about his sexual exploits with Snow. That was none of their fucking business.

Brooklyn and Chance planted themselves in the middle of the floor like oak trees as they anticipated the details.

They wore sneaky grins on their faces as they were yanked back into the moment when they too had Selena.

With the proper audience in play, scrawny Rasim placed his hands in front of him like he was holding the girl's waist and was sexing her from the back. "So I had her like this, right," he moved his hips back and forth in a foolish manner. "And she was like, 'More, more, Papi. Your dick so big. Your dick so fat.'"

"She did me like that too," Brooklyn contributed, barely able to remain still.

"I'm telling you that shit was so tight and wet," Rasim continued as he snatched the mic and regained control of the floor. "So I smacked her ass and was like—"

When Brooklyn and Chance's expressions changed from delight to alarm suddenly, Rasim wondered what horror awaited him. When he followed their gaze with a slow roll of his head toward the door, he was staring into the hazel browns of the love of his young life...Snow.

Snow was rooted in her position as tears filled the wells of her eyes and threatened to drown her on the spot. She loved Rasim with all that God had given her. Her body. Her mind. And her soul. Why did he require more?

Humiliated beyond belief, her bottom lip twitched as she turned to make an exit. Unlike when she left Morris's closet, this time Snow caught wheels as she sped away with what was left of her broken heart.

Rasim, on the other hand, was stuck. His limbs were stiff and the beat of his heart could be seen through the black Polo shirt he donned. His mouth stayed open and his nose burned. He was breathing so heavily he was on the verge of overheating. He could even feel himself wanting to weep although he would never allow such a graceful act in front of his compadres.

Instead, he flopped down on Southeast Brian's bed even though he didn't play that shit on his own bed, and threw his face into his hands.

He fucked up.

It was official.

Snow Bradshaw had left the building.

Forever.

Rasim did all he could to conduct a search party to locate her but nothing worked. He even tried to sneak into Ms. Brush Face's office to get Snow's address and got caught. She cursed him out with fifty different words, most of them in Spanish. But she liked the young boy, which was the only reason she didn't give him a harsh punishment. Besides, even a woman with a face like hers understood real love. She just wasn't prepared to lose her job for him.

Although Rasim conducted his investigation, he did it without alerting his homies. He wanted them to think that he couldn't care less that Snow had kicked rocks. Even though both bore witness to the mental breakdown he exhibited when he was caught.

Fuck he want with a Church Girl when he had access to Selena and Queen, who just sucked his dick after music class earlier that day? He was Rasim Nami, a player, nothing more and nothing less.

He was good on the love shit, he told them in several meetings, even though he wanted to talk about Snow during every free chance he got. But all he spoke were lies.

With each day that passed where he didn't see his beautiful Snow, he lost a bit of his mind. He lost a little bit of his heart and even a few pounds he couldn't spare.

Finally, on the second week, Brooklyn and Chance couldn't take it anymore. Rasim had taken to staying in his bedroom and looking at the pictures he'd taken of Snow while she was there. It was a sad spectacle to behold and even a few hardened delinquents had to get away from Rasim for fear they'd shed a noble tear.

No, Brooklyn and Chance had to stop their friend's pain at once. In a private meeting, they elected to either help him or kill him and put him out of his misery. Luckily for Rasim, they chose the first option.

With a decision in place, Chance decided to ask Mute Candy for Snow's address. But she cursed him out so badly he was five seconds from saying fuck Snow and her mother too.

When he acquainted Brooklyn with her poor manners, he didn't believe him. He figured a mute couldn't possibly be as bad as Chance made out and he decided to give it a whirl. But true to his word, he received exactly what Chance got. High-flying hands and a wide mouth, which was horrifying although void of sound.

The duo was right. Snow had shared information with her but Mute Candy had no intentions on helping any of the varlets. She did not approve of how Rasim treated her friend and she expressed it using her body language and passion.

It was true. Mute Candy didn't say a word. Then again, she didn't need to.

After Mute Candy's wrath, in another attempt to restore their brother's heart, who made them laugh daily, it was time to step up their game. So they placed a laxative in

Ms. Brush Face's coffee, which sent her to the Porcelain God for two days straight, thereby giving them full access to her office.

When they had the information they needed, they approached Rasim from the back as he sat in the cafeteria looking stupid. It wasn't even lunchtime.

"Rasim, you good?" Brooklyn asked already knowing the answer. He and Chance perched next to him.

"I'm straight," he said as he stared into space. The poor lad was overcome with grief.

Chance couldn't take it anymore. Although Brooklyn preferred to drag shit out by withholding details, he reached into his pocket, removed a small white sheet of paper and slid Snow's information toward him across the table.

Rasim didn't bother to look at it. He was uninterested. "What is it?"

"Snow's address. Now go get your bitch."

CHAPTER 7

SNOW

S now leaned against her mother's warm arm as she listened to the preacher conduct his powerful sermon from the pulpit.

A sad cloud hovered over the Bradshaw family, that was for sure.

Maureen clutched her daughter's warm hand as if she were recharging her with all of the love she lost while at Strawberry Meadows. By the grace of God, Snow was allowed an early release because of her pregnancy and it felt good to be around her parents and their strength.

Maureen didn't know what was troubling Snow, neither did her father for that matter, but they made it clear that they had her back. And that even if the world attempted to besiege her, there would always be love for Snow in their home.

If the truth be told, then this also must be said. Lamont was a religious man who, when he announced he loved the Lord, meant it with every fiber of his being. But, he would just as soon commit mass homicide if anybody shaved a hair on gentle Snow's head and then await his chariot to hell.

Besides, the agony they felt having to take Snow to an abortion clinic was enormous. They essentially assisted in the murder of their first grandchild and they weren't feeling it one bit. But Snow had big dreams and she felt a child might get in the way. Moreover, after hearing Rasim carry on about another girl, she didn't want to birth his baby anyway. He never even said he loved her.

In that way, Snow was stronger than most teenagers her age who would have carried the baby just to keep a connection with its father.

Had it not been for the fact that Snow said the young man didn't know about her pregnancy, Lamont would've hit it to Strawberry Meadows '70s Gangster style.

The strategy would've been quite simple really. He would've yanked the boy out of the home by way of his vocal cords, placed a *cool* barrel to his head and demonstrated how quickly it *heated* up. And all anybody watching could say would be, "Poor Rasim".

Luckily for Rasim, that was unnecessary, for when Lamont gazed into Snow's eyes he knew she was in love. And for a doting father, for the moment anyway, that would simply have to do.

When Rasim's beautiful face infiltrated Snow's mind again her heart ached, *literally*. It was like some weird contractions that made it difficult to breathe. Was she having a heart attack? Was she about to die? Why was she forced to see his face disappear and reappear as if on repeat?

It hurt too fucking much!

Make it stop!

Frustrated, she slammed her eyes shut and tried to push the pain away from her spirit. Placing her free hand over her chest, she demanded that either God bring him back to her at once, or strike any existence of him from her mind. *Forever*.

The pain.

Oh the pain!

It was pure agony and yet that was not a strong enough word.

All Snow could do was relinquish power over to God and allow Him to heal her. Loving Rasim was not strong enough to overcome the soreness of losing him. She didn't want to feel this type of suffering again.

With her lids still closed, she felt her body trembling at volcanic levels. She was about to cry and beg the preacher to lay hands on her soul when suddenly someone lifted her hand and gripped it tightly.

Was it God? Did He come down Himself to save her life? To heal her broken heart?

Slowly Snow's eyes peeled open and Rasim was staring at her. He had also been given an early release as long as his father promised to guide his path. Why, at that very moment Mr. Nami stood in back of the church as a testament of his support.

Snow blinked a few times because this could not be real. If it were an evil joke, she would not be able to survive afterwards.

But if it was real...if he was really there, what a beautiful way to heal her broken heart.

Snow wasn't the only one looking at the young man. He had also stolen Lamont and Maureen's attention. Each of them held a pocket full of choice words with his name on it but now was not the time or place to make the delivery. The young man made an intelligent move by reentering their daughter's world in the house of the Lord and for now he would maintain the stage and his life.

Rasim, who didn't place a toenail in the mosque in Strawberry Meadows, walked into the Baptist church for his precious Snow. Even Slack Jaw Morris had to clutch his collared shirt because the love in Rasim's eyes was so strong.

"I'm sorry," he whispered as a single tear rolled down his cheek. He didn't care how soft he looked at the moment. He didn't care what people watching thought of him either. He would not live another day without Snow Bradshaw in his life. "I apologize for hurting your feelings. But I'm begging you not to leave me." He gripped her hand harder to the point of creating pain. "Please, baby. Please forgive me and give me one more chance. I love you."

"I can't do it," she shook her head. "It's too hard."

Rasim was horrified upon hearing her response. He hadn't expected her answer. "One more chance is all I ask. Just one. Isn't it worth it for the sake of love?"

Flooded with love, she wrapped her arms around his slender body and squeezed tightly. Her nose rested in the pit of his neck and she inhaled his cologne.

Yes.

He was her man.

He was her Rasim.

Through no fault of their own, they had successfully gained the audience of the faculty, usher board and congregation.

But who cared?

They were in love.

And they would forever be entwined.

But a dark cloud was coming to test their love, for which they were not prepared.

CHAPTER 8

MAY 2014
WASHINGTON, DC

PRESENT DAY

Alf Herman sat in the wooden chair in the foyer in awe. The story of how they met was so inspiring that even he got emotional. But still, he couldn't understand why he was sitting in the middle of the living room watching blood drip from the Officer's body. He wasn't moving as much as he had been and Alf was concerned.

"Your story is inspiring," he yelled to be heard beyond the doors. "So I take it that you are Rasim."

Silence.

"I am."

"And who is the man on the steps bleeding?"

"We haven't finished telling you the story," Snow interrupted.

"My apologies." He moved uncomfortably in his seat and observed the police officer again. "It's just that time is not on our side. A man is dying."

She giggled. "People kill me with that statement." She paused. "That time is not on our side. Time is a beautiful thing actually. It gives men an opportunity to correct that which is wrong. It offers them a chance to stop hurting those they claim to love. But for me, it did so much more."

"What do you mean?" Alf Herman replied.

"Rasim always wanted to rule but my heart wasn't a big enough country. He had to have it all. He had to sit on the throne even if it meant wasting his time on places or people unworthy. All while ignoring me in the process." She paused. "It's funny though. Because I knew something he didn't."

"And what's that?"

"That even the mighty fall."

PARTTWO

BY T. STYLES

CHAPTER 9

SNOW

FEBRUARY 2001

Snow's black high-heeled boot pressed against the gas pedal as she zoomed up the highway on the way to Hains Point in Washington, DC. One hand clutched the steering wheel of her red Audi and the other gripped her belly. She was devastated because although he promised not to, Rasim hurt her once again.

When she received the news that he was seen in Selena's black Suburban, she was on her way home to prepare Rasim's dinner. The whistleblower sounded Latina and she was sure it was Selena's funky ass.

What was wrong with him? Why was she never enough?

Although she attended the University of Maryland Dance Academy where she studied dance during the week, while Rasim sold dope on the streets, she made sure his meals were prepared every night. And this was how he elected to repay her? With public humiliation?

When she assessed herself in the mirror, she couldn't believe the sight. The mascara from her lashes smeared around her eyes, giving her a panda bear effect. Let's not even talk about the condition of her light skin. It turned a shade of red not yet created in the dictionary.

It seemed like every other month, if he wasn't in jail for bullshit, he was spotted with some bitch who thought because he looked exotic she had to see if his cum was sweet.

Miserable bitches!

Miserable Rasim!

For the past six years Snow had proven to be a good bitch. A real loyal bitch who didn't pledge allegiance to the flag but to his dick.

And when Rasim found himself in the crack game, it was Snow who helped him cook in between her classes. She was beside herself with anger. He spoke of loyalty often. But what good was it to rep loyalty when the words held no weight?

When she made a right onto Ohio Drive in southwest DC, she followed the signs into Hains Point. The water, which enclosed the park, shimmered when kissed with sunlight. Any other time, it would be beautiful but the way Snow felt, she considered running her car into the icy Potomac River.

"God, I love this man," she prayed. "I know you see my heart. Please don't let what I'm told be true."

As she steered her car around the perimeter of the park, it wasn't long before she spotted Selena's black Suburban. It was in full bling mode parked near the Awakening sculpture. The art showcased a man who appeared to be climbing out of the ground.

Snow clutched the steering wheel tighter and pressed her foot harder on the gas. When she was closer, she parked any kind of way, jumped out, left her door open and shuffled toward the truck with clenched fists. Snow didn't fight but she allowed her body to move as if she wanted to.

She stomped harder than the most thorough marching band down south.

But soon her courage was gone. Because as she peered through the windshield, she witnessed her man in the passenger seat with his head hung back and his lids closed. Although it appeared that the driver's seat was empty, she knew the real deal. Gone were the days of complete naivety. Snow was smart as a whip.

Damn, them niggas slipping. What if I was the police?

Wanting to catch him in the act, she lowered her body and crept toward the passenger side. When she was upon the truck she banged heavily on the window with intentions to break it.

But her mouth fell open when she saw Selena's jaws wrapped around her dude's dick like a glove. Seeing his lady's face, Rasim shoved the Latina by way of her forehead so that he could hop out and beg for Snow's mercy.

However, Selena had other ideas. Behind Rasim's back she grinned at Snow, turned the truck on and whipped it to the right as she fled the scene with Rasim in tow.

Confused, Snow darted into the middle of the street in an attempt to catch the truck but Selena was ghost.

Snow dropped to her knees and sobbed uncontrollably as she pounded the pavement so hard her hands bled.

The fireplace crackled as Snow curled up in a ball on her mother. She was sobbing uncontrollably into her breasts as Maureen rubbed her back. Snow was in full baby mode.

PRISON THRONE

This had become such a common affair that although Maureen didn't want her daughter hurting, she had grown slightly unsympathetic to the issue. "I don't know what else to do, mama," she said as her tears dampened her mother's shirt. "I love him so much but he doesn't love me back. He doesn't care how much he hurts me or how he makes me feel!"

Of course Maureen didn't like the way Rasim was treating Snow but she also knew she went through the same thing with Lamont. So who was she to point a hypocritical finger?

"You know Rasim loves you, Snow. But you gave him the key to your heart. So you don't own it anymore," she schooled. "The way I see it, is like this, you have two options and you must choose wisely. Either deal with the women that he will continue to have in his life," she gently touched her face, "or leave. The outcome, although not easy, is totally up to you."

Huffing and puffing, Snow rose up and looked into her mother's eyes. "Can I move in here for a little while?"

"No," her father said walking from behind the sofa. He wasn't home at first and he moved so lightly, a skill he learned from his gangster days, that no one ever heard him coming before he wanted them to.

Lamont sat his suitcase on the sofa and lowered his head to kiss his wife before pecking Snow also.

Maureen, beside herself with anger, smeared her husband's affection away. "What do you mean no?" Maureen asked with a lowered brow. "Our daughter asked could she stay and it is our duty to protect her."

"No it's not, honey," he corrected her, placing a gray clump of hair behind her ear. "It is our duty to ensure that she never runs away from her problems." He looked over at Snow whose nose was beet red. "Sweetheart, you're twenty-two-years-old now. You can't run anymore. Now if you want to be with this young man, then you're going to have to deal with the good and the bad. Once you've tried it all, and I see it in your eyes, then you're free to come back home. But not a moment sooner."

Snow was pushing a cart through Giant Grocery Store with a list in her hand. She had stared at it so long that suddenly she couldn't read it.

Mute Candy, who had proven to be a champion in Snow's life, removed the list from her hand and quarterbacked the shopping for the day.

As Mute Candy placed item after item into the cart, Snow suddenly doubled over and cried out. The pain she felt courtesy of Rasim's latest Selena adventure was just too much. She felt as if her intestines were being rolled into a ball and stomped on. Her heart burned and her temples throbbed and when she tried to pull herself together, she felt paralyzed as she slapped onto the grungy floor.

Even Mute Candy, who didn't cry for shit, dropped three tears.

When twin brothers, who were also body builders, saw the condition the young lady was in, they abandoned their cart stuffed with the finest meats, and ran to the dame's rescue. "Is she okay?" one of them asked Mute Candy, staring at Snow with concerned eyes.

But because she couldn't speak, she whipped out a pen and pad and wrote down her concerns.

PRISON THRONE

The older brother with arms like Hercules read her words. *She has a broken heart. Can you help her to the car?*

Without another written word, one of the brothers scooped her up like she weighed a pound and escorted her toward the exit. Once outside, Snow was situated in the passenger seat of her Audi. Mute Candy thanked both men by way of a nod and a sincere smile before they left to finish their shopping.

Rasim getting on my fucking nerves! Mute Candy thought.

She was tiring of the way he treated her friend.

Mute Candy slid into the driver's seat and studied Snow whose face was bloody red. Tears poured out of her eyes and dampened the collar of her shirt. Snow resembled a baby who drank juice without a bib.

Mute Candy touched her leg and tried to think of a formula to sign to make her friend feel better. But was one invented for the woman with a severed heart? If it was, she didn't know the words.

So she simply rubbed her leg empathetically, located the list and completed Snow's chore. Once again, as always really, Mute Candy made the right move. She decided to allow her friend the time to cry until she couldn't anymore as she finished shopping.

Mute Candy was so valuable to Snow's heart that Snow not only learned sign language but she mastered it. Once a month, she taught the language at a community college for free. Even Mute Candy learned a thing or two from Snow because she was that good.

When Mute Candy first left the group home and reconnected with Snow, Snow assumed there weren't many people in Mute Candy's life but that wasn't the case. Although Diane Dallas was so far in the streets that she had become like a brick to a project building, there were many who loved Mute Candy, most of whom were her cousins.

Every last one of them learned sign language or a variation thereof because when Mute Candy loved, she loved hard and everyone benefited. Her love coupled with her super hero syndrome made her interesting to say the least.

Though she had many favorites, none was closer to her than Snow Bradshaw and that went for family too.

They were kindred spirits when you looked at it. Mute Candy didn't speak because she couldn't and Snow remained speechless because she could. As a result, they always understood one another.

Once Mute Candy finished shopping, she drove her best friend home. She didn't try to communicate but wanted Snow to know that no matter what, she cared about her. Their bond exceeded the boundaries of this world.

So when Snow was halfway to her destination, she wiped her wet face, turned her head slowly and said, "I love you too."

Mute Candy grinned and piloted the car home.

CHAPTER 10

RASIM

Rasim's temples pumped major blood as he sat in the passenger seat of Selena's truck while she drove. When she sped away from his beautiful Snow at Hains Point without giving him the chance to talk to her, he contemplated doing what he did not respect, fracturing a female's jaw.

But as Selena continued to navigate the ride, he went somewhere else mentally. It was almost surreal. Suddenly he was standing in the middle of the street begging for Snow's love but just like that she vanished before his eyes.

Rasim had pushed the boundaries of hell with this latest move. Sure he fucked a bitch or two. And yes, Snow caught a number dangling out of his pocket when he got too drunk to record it in his phone and throw it away. But up until this moment she never, ever, caught him in the act.

How he wished he hadn't left his silver BMW 3 Series in front of his parents' house. He could've bounced on that dumb bitch a long time ago. But Selena enjoyed when she squired Rasim about town in her car because she could keep him longer, so he was at her temporary mercy. Plus Rasim's dick was the biggest she ever had and she loved that most of all about him.

When Rasim saw Benning Road train station ahead he said, "Pull over." It was the first thing he uttered to the bitch since she yanked him from Snow.

"Rasim, I know you not mad at me," Selena confronted in a flair that only a sassy Latina could master. With one finger up, she swayed it back and forth like a windshield wiper. "It's not my fault that bitch—"

She wanted to finish her sentence but who could with the glare he threw her way? It was a serious one too, one that could lead to a face pounding or a murder if Selena said just one more thing. If she wanted to survive, it was best that she grew as silent as a rock.

"If you ever disrespect Snow and call her out her name again, I can't make any promises on what I might do to you," he warned.

When he looked at her chin he saw a drop of his sperm resting nicely. In her haste she didn't get a chance to lick it off. Had she not been such a sneaky underhanded bitch, he would've alerted her so that she could erase it from her face before returning to her precious husband. But after the shit she pulled, he'd just as soon say, "Fuck you, bitch," and keep it moving.

When the truck stopped, Rasim started to call Donald and ask him to come scoop him up since they slang dope not too far from the station. Instead he opted to take the train, which would allow him time to think.

His stomach grumbled when he saw Snow's face again in his mind.

What the fuck is wrong with me? He thought. *I'm about to lose the best thing I ever had.*

If an outsider assessed the matter, they would assume that he didn't love her but they would be so wrong. He adored her more than he knew how to express. But there was something about Selena that had him feeling silly at times. She was like a good bag of chips. Although he desperately tried, he couldn't eat just one.

PRISON THRONE

Sexy, freaky, slutty, spontaneous and all of the above could be used to describe her. You could also add sneaky, conniving and slick if you wanted to compile a proper list. Whatever her appeal, he couldn't shake her and he cursed the Gods for the power she held over his dick.

It wasn't even like she was available. She married a mechanic and had a kid by him. Not only that, Selena stood Rasim up so many times he was starting to think she didn't fuck with him anymore. It was also rumored by a few hood boys that she said that although Rasim was as cute as baby lips, he wasn't a man's man. He wasn't an alpha! Which was what she was attracted to.

So after he reached out and she wouldn't return his call, he would allow thoughts of her to evaporate and that's when she would call with something like, "I'm trying to fuck," to break his resolve.

This shit was a mess! Of gigantic proportions and he didn't see a good ending to the melodrama coming his way.

⚕⚕ ⚕⚕

Since his car was out in front of his parents' house, Rasim decided to visit with them first before going home. Lately things changed with the Nami family.

Over the years his father adopted rigid beliefs and it scared Rasim because he never knew the source of his aggression. When Rasim was coming up, Kamran was always supportive and loving and now he was militant and serious. As a result, they didn't click anymore and it broke Rasim's heart. But it didn't stop him from loving him.

Before Rasim walked into his parents' house, out of respect, he took a moment to slip on his Kufi, which was nothing more than a glorified costume.

When he was dressed, he bopped inside with the wide smile on his face that melted the hearts of women up and down the coast. But when he saw his mother, his blood pressure skyrocketed and the grin fell off.

Umar was sitting on the sofa, her face crimson. She had been crying so much that the light hijab she wore was mottled with tearstains.

Beside himself with fear, he rushed over to her and dropped to his knees so that they were at eye level.

What the fuck was going on in his world?

He could take a lot of things but seeing the two women he adored more than time and space weeping in the same day was too much for even Hitler to bear.

"Mama," he said gripping her shoulders, trying desperately not to apply too much pressure, "what's wrong? Is papa okay?"

She shook her wet face slowly. "No, my dear boy. It's gotten worse."

"What happened? Tell me," he demanded.

Umar leaned in so that Rasim could hear her clearly. "I'm afraid he is involved with Al-Qaeda." With that, she leaned back and her lips trembled.

Rasim's rear slapped to the floor with the news. He didn't know much about the militant group but he did know they didn't fuck with America, the country he had grown to love.

The basics went like this. Al-Qaeda, which means "the base" in Arabic, is the network for extremists organized by Osama Bin Laden of Saudi Arabia. The organiza-

PRISON THRONE

tion got its roots when natives attempted to rise against the Soviet occupation of Afghanistan.

Thousands of mujahideen (warriors) came from the Middle East and, fortunately for these warriors, Osama had money to fund the war. The mujahedeen won against the Soviet Union and they all had Osama's moneybags to thank.

Feeling like a "G" since they defeated the Soviet forces, Osama went back to Saudi Arabia and funded an organization to help wounded soldiers. He was like a God to thousands of brave men.

With the win under his belt, Osama felt more powerful. So when Iraq invaded Kuwait in 1990 and his government allowed US troops to be stationed in Saudi Arabia, he went ballistic. He didn't think Americans should be allowed to set up shop in the birthplace of Islam. But not all of his people were feeling his views and they kicked his ass out of his own country for anti-government activities.

After he was dismissed from his own land, after all he had done, Osama set up an Al-Qaeda shop (which most believe already existed) in Sudan and declared war against the US. Since he realized he couldn't run the operation alone, he recruited a few rich bosses and they multiplied in numbers, money and power.

At the end of the day, the primary focus of Al-Qaeda was to drive Americans and American influence out of all Muslim nations. He also wanted to unite all Muslims, which was how Rasim's father got pulled in.

Although evil, Osama was smart. He gained control using man's most precious possession, his love for God.

At the end of the day Osama wanted all Muslims to follow the first caliphs. Under this order it is the duty of Muslims around the world to wage holy war on the U.S.,

American citizens and Jews. And any Muslim who failed to heed the call would be declared an apostate (someone who has forsaken his faith).

Rasim looked up at his mother upon hearing the devastating news. Kamran's connection with Al-Qaeda explained why he had been acting so strange lately. He was possessed. "Where is he now, ma?" Rasim asked softly.

"Downstairs," she pointed at the door leading to the basement. "With them."

Rasim stood up and wandered over. Before entering he observed his mother once more. For some reason he felt as if life as he knew it would change forever, so something in his heart desired to savor his mother's beautiful face.

When he was as ready as he was going to get, he walked down two steps and stopped when he heard voices. He wanted to remain out of view. With his ear hustling game intact, he observed the men speaking in Urdu, a language of Pakistani people and his father. Rasim wasn't too fluent but he did understand the words 'plane' and 'hostage' very well. But how did they connect?

When the stairs made a creaking sound, the men ceased talking and Kamran rushed to the foot of the steps only to see his son's guilty expression.

Thanks to Rasim, the meeting was adjourned.

When all of the men with features that resembled Rasim's exited the home, he and his father were left alone.

Now Rasim and his pops sat face to face in silence. Usually when they were this close Kamran would touch his son out of love but everything changed. His expression was so hardened that he couldn't formulate a smile if he desired to.

Rasim looked down at his hands that were clutched in front of him. "Dad, don't do it." He didn't have any details but he could tell by the dark air the men left that something was awry.

Kamran frowned. "You can't ask me what you choose to ignore," he said calmly.

"What does that mean?"

"War is upon us, son. Which side are you on?"

"Dad, you don't know what you're doing." His voice was high pitched. "You and ma are computer analysts. Not soldiers."

Kamran was insulted. His lips tightened. "Do you think just because you wear your Kufi costume when you're in my home that you have the right to talk to me about my beliefs?"

Mental shots were fired.

"Dad, I'm not saying that," Rasim exhaled. "And I'm sorry that I haven't embraced the religion and the customs of our people like you have. But it doesn't mean that I don't have a right to love you." Rasim decided he would no longer sit so close to his father and not express his love so he touched the top of his hand. "Dad, I'm begging you, whatever you're planning please don't do it. Think about me, your only son, and ma."

When Rasim saw his father's cheek bubble on the left side he knew that he was suppressing a cry. But instead of allowing the weight of Al-Qaeda to release itself from his shoulders, he swallowed it again.

Angry with Rasim for stirring up his emotions, he jumped up and said, "As long as you continue to deny Muslim beliefs and the damage that this country has caused to yours, you are not welcome in my home. Now leave!"

Rasim's eyes widened as he heard the words he never thought his father would ever say to him.

Fuck no he wasn't leaving!

BY T. STYLES

Kamran was his man and he loved him!

So instead of bouncing, he rose and snatched his father into an embrace. For a second Kamran didn't push back. But as if the levees were suddenly broken on a dam, he shoved Rasim with so much force that he toppled over the chair.

"Leave, Rasim," Kamran warned pointing at the steps. "Your mother and I never want to see you again. If you choose not to, the next thing you hear will be the clap of my gun."

Rasim sat in his BMW for an hour outside of his home. He heard the saying that you make your bed and you have to lie in it but there was a flaw. Rasim had two beds. One he made with Selena and the other that Al-Qaeda created. So where would he sleep?

This was all too confusing. First he had to deal with his parents and now it was time to handle Snow. Today just wasn't his fucking day.

As he leaned back in his seat he thought about how sad Snow looked earlier and could only derive that at the moment she was an emotional wreck, especially since he hadn't called.

Normally he would blow her phone up when he was caught cheating but considering his father and the mess he had gotten himself into, well, simply put, Rasim didn't have any verve to spare.

When he realized Snow needed him too he exited the car and strutted to the tiny home they owned off of South Dakota Avenue.

The moment he opened the door to his house he saw the table set with fried chicken, rice and spinach, but it was Mute Candy who was the chef.

Snow was balled up on the couch sound asleep.

Aw shit! She was bound to be a handful.

Rasim hung in the doorway and refrained from taking another step inside of his own home. He knew how Mute Candy felt about Snow. The world did. Her feelings were almost as strong as his but not quite.

With a serious attitude problem and with eyes on Rasim the entire time, Mute Candy snatched her leather coat off the chair and punched each arm into the holes. For added flair, she snatched her purse off the table and threw it over her shoulder so hard it slapped against her back and she burped. With her items in order, she stomped toward Rasim and scrutinized his eyes.

When she held back long enough, she slapped him on the right side of his face and proceeded to the left. With his face burning red, she tilted her head, pointed aggressively at her cheek and he bent down and kissed it.

"I love you too," he said because it was true.

Mute Candy stomped out of the house leaving him and his girl alone.

Her antics may have seemed bad but Rasim knew the only other person on the planet earth who loved Snow as much as he did was Mute Candy. He was lucky she chose the method of slapping him as opposed to anything else. Why, just last Christmas, Bernard Miller from Bladensburg, Maryland, found himself in front of her car when he hurt her cousin's feelings. So Rasim was grateful.

When Mute Candy left, Snow was sitting on the sofa with her legs pressed against her chest. She looked over at him. She looked like a little girl who just received the news that both her parents and best friend were killed in the same day. Always at Rasim's beck and call, she asked, "You want me to make your plate?" Her voice was subdued.

"No, baby," he swallowed. "I can't eat a thing."

Rasim maneuvered his tall body toward her slowly. When he stood above her, he reduced his height so that he was looking directly into her eyes. Since it was widely known that Snow did limited talking, especially when she had to express her feelings, he moved to kiss her without asking. Her feet fell to the rug and she pushed him with a shove of her tiny fist.

He didn't give a fuck though.

She was his bitch and it was time to beg until his knees bled.

So Rasim attempted to kiss her again and this time she used her knee to press his lanky body out of the way. However, Rasim of Pakistan was nothing if not persistent.

"I'm sorry," he whispered kissing her softly on the cheek. This time he nailed it.

"Stop," she said so softly her voice was almost undetectable.

"I'm sorry," he mumbled as he kissed her neck.

With each peck, he apologized until her face was covered and he kissed each tear away. Since he had begged a thousand pardons it was only fitting to kiss her eyelids next. "I'm so fucking sorry, baby," he repeated as he removed the gray University of Maryland Dance Academy sweatshirt she wore.

Snow tried to fight but it was no use. The only thing she wanted in the world was Rasim. The humans on Planet Earth could keep everything else.

PRISON THRONE

Rasim was so sorrowful that he chanted "I'm sorry" as if it were an ancient incantation that would make her forget how Selena suckled his dick hours earlier.

He was passionate and he wanted Snow to know that he would cut off his hands if he were sure it would stop the lust he had in his body for Selena. "Hit me," he begged.

"No, Rasim," she whispered.

He aggressively gripped her wrists and got in her face. "Hit me, bitch."

It was amazing!

He said the magic words with the proper power and Snow slapped him so many times his bottom lip cracked open and bled. Suddenly she was crying again.

Bloodied and bruised, he said, "I love you."

Snow couldn't hit him anymore so she spit in his face.

He didn't wipe it away. He let it remain because she put it there.

"I love you," he said again gazing into her eyes.

She spit harder and it dropped on his bottom lip and he licked it off.

Passionately she snatched his face against hers and kissed the blood off of his mouth.

When she was done, Rasim chanted repeatedly how sorry he was and by the time he was finished he kissed her out of her clothing and she was laid before him on the floor naked. As he stood on his knees and observed her beautiful body, he felt like shit. How could he keep treating his angel so poorly?

Snow's hazel eyes looked upon him with mercy. All she desired was for him to stop breaking her heart. Stop making her cry and stop allowing other women to touch what was rightfully hers. His body.

BY T. STYLES

"I'd give you my soul if you would just promise to stop hurting me, Rasim," she wept as her body convulsed. "I just can't take it anymore. Have mercy on me. I'm begging you."

Now it was Rasim who was choking up. He wiped his tears away with his wrist, grabbed the comforter she was using off of the couch and put it over her body so that she would be warm.

He stooped down and kissed her lips, "I'm so sorry, baby. That bitch doesn't mean anything to me and I will never hurt you again."

Her mind maintained that his tongue spoke lies but her heart rejoiced. Whether or not it was true, for the moment anyway, it felt so damn good.

Rasim lowered his body and gently spread her legs apart. He could smell the faint musty odor stemming from her pussy but it was not offensive in the least. It just meant she had been a wreck since she left dance class and, thanks to his bullshit, she didn't have time to shower.

Even if she smelled of the foulest sea, he would still kiss her until she was all clean. Because he was certain that, if nothing else, he was the only man who had ever entered her body, which was more than he could say for Selena the Siren.

He placed his partially open mouth over her pussy and blew a blast of warm air onto her clit. He liked to heat up her button before he did his thing and she loved it too.

"Piss on my face, Snow," he ordered.

"No, Rasim," she whispered and tried to clamp her thighs together.

He slapped them apart again and his red handprint presented itself on her skin. The only time Rasim agreed

PRISON THRONE

with beating women was in the bed and Snow secretly loved it.

"Piss on me," he demanded more aggressively.

Fuck that nigga! She thought.

If he wanted it, she would let him have it. So she relaxed her body and pissed all over Rasim's face, drenching the carpeted floor beneath them.

He wanted to be degraded.

He wanted to be punished.

When she was finished, she felt eerily vindicated but Rasim was far from done. He blew warm breaths into her pussy again until she was as hot as a furnace. He lapped his tongue repeatedly over her clit. Up and down, left and right until her syrup was oozing into his mouth.

"Rasim," she wept, "I love you so fucking much." Snow was crying real tears, not tears of joy and that fucked with Rasim's head.

It hurt his heart to know that because of the shit he did on the street, he had broken his angel's heart yet again.

Worried she was on the verge of cumming too soon, he stopped laboring on her clit. Instead he entered her warm tunnel with his stiff tongue recurrently, until she was clenching his ears like handles and bucking her hips wildly.

Rasim was skinny but he knew how to beg and fuck. That was for sure.

After fifteen minutes, when he'd given her tunnel the proper observation, he revisited her clit again. Rasim's dick was so swollen and erect that it was uncomfortable to lie on his belly so he reached into his jeans, shifted that bitch to the right and proceeded to handle his business.

Not being able to enter her was torture!

BY T. STYLES

As much as he wanted to bury himself inside of Snow's body, this shit was not about him. It was all about his sweet baby.

However, in a surprising turn of events, Snow was so wet and Rasim was so turned on that he was able to rub one out on the floor anyway. It was the first time he was able to cum like that but he would never forget it. Without the benefit of entering her body, she still satisfied him.

Amazing.

Rasim was even more passionate as he gripped her thighs and buried his face so deep into her mound that, before long, Snow exploded over his lips. Even though she begged him to stop because her clit was tender, Rasim licked and licked until all of her juices were gone and that's when he really went to work on her.

The morning dropped by when Rasim finally stopped. And it was only because his jaw was so stiff it was discomforting and she couldn't cum anymore if she tried.

That was the best begging he had done in his life and he only hoped she could feel his heart and feel his sincere apology.

He regretted hurting her.

He truly did.

Rasim had to hit the blocks to get his paper but he didn't want to leave her.

He was still between her legs when he looked up and asked, "Can I stay here a little longer?"

She smiled because she was so worn out that she didn't want to go to dance class either. "Yes, Rasim," she whispered.

So he lowered his head and took a nap right next to Snow's pussy.

PRISON THRONE

CHAPTER 11

RASIM

It was a gray day and the sun was hiding behind chunky clouds. God was threatening the young hustlers with rain. Rasim, Donald, Brooklyn and Chance were standing against a fence in front of a building within the projects, waiting to serve customers.

Although the sky would most likely open up and spill water, the day was actually heavy with possibilities. Earlier Donald received a call from Phantom, their boss, and it sounded promising. If shit worked out, he could earn more money, which meant an increase for them all.

Rasim was ecstatic for Donald because over the six years after the rape charge, he couldn't seem to catch a break. He was in prison for a year and came out lost and confused. It wasn't until Sheila was mysteriously found with her neck slit open that Donald was blessed with a bout of good luck.

For starters, he married a girl who reached out to him on a pen pal site and wrote him frequently while he was locked down. When he came home they had twin girls and everyone said he seemed more relaxed since he was a dad. He didn't pop off the handle much anymore and all he could talk about was his kids every free second he got. He wanted to be the parent he never had and he did an out-standing job. Everyone surmised that even a wild bear could show love to its cubs.

If he received the raise from pawn to lieutenant, he would be able to help his wife, who held a government job, with the expenses. He would save his paper, buy his family a nicer home and move them from DC to Maryland.

"Who fucked you up?" Chanced joked looking at Rasim's mouth. Snow had thrashed him something fierce and it showed.

His homies looked at him and awaited an answer.

"Your mama's fat ass," he winked.

Everyone chuckled.

"Man, I can't stay still," Donald said as he continued to look up the block for Phantom's car. "Where this nigga at?" He looked at the watch on his arm. He stuffed his hands in his jacket.

"I don't know why you worried," Brooklyn responded as he leaned against the fence, making it squeak. Over the years, he lost a few pounds, which he converted into muscle, and during the summer months he would fake spill some shit on himself to gain a reason to take off his shirt and flex his muscles. The bitches loved it but his homies hated the show. "You got that. You already know." He slipped his hood over his head.

"Right, who else gonna get it?" Chance asked as he served a chick he fucked once in high school who was so skinny he almost didn't recognize her. "Me?" He pointed to himself. "Or that fake ass exhibitionist to your right?"

"Fuck you," Brooklyn said.

"What about me?" Rasim joked as he popped a few sunflower seeds into his mouth.

"Ain't nobody hiring your Afghan ass to do nothing but find Saddam Hussein," Chance responded with a corny joke he was known for. "I know you got his number, don't you? Tell the truth."

Rasim wore a smile but he was sure getting tired of people bringing up Hussein whenever he was around. He did all he could to look like his friends, including stuffing his Kufi in his pocket, wearing baseball caps and hiding most of his face. Most of the time, he looked Indian or black. But at the end of the day they always reminded him about who he really was...Pakistani. And he didn't know who to hate more because of it. Himself for neglecting his religion and people, or his friends.

"I'm not trying to hear that shit," Rasim said as he pretended to busy himself with the phone in his pocket. "How 'bout you check under your mama's gut for the nigga." He paused knowing his parents owned a bakery and Chance's mother was overweight. "That bitch eat more product than she sell."

The young men spent another ten minutes laughing and disrespecting each other's mothers until Donald said, "Rasim, go get me some Hennessy from up the street. My nerves gonna be bad unless I get a drink."

"Aight," he said as he zipped his jacket.

"I'm going with him," Brooklyn said.

"I don't give a fuck, nigga," Donald responded.

He gave Rasim the money and he and Brooklyn bopped up the street to the liquor store. Neighborhood rock stars since day one, they waved at the locals on the way to their destination. They talked about their girlfriends and how Rasim got caught with Selena again and how he was really done with her this time. Brooklyn heard all the shit before but he was reminded of something when he heard Selena's name.

"Hey, you ever see her kid?"

Rasim frowned. "Naw, why you ask that?"

"Because I swear he looks slam like you, slim."

BY T. STYLES

Rasim chuckled as they dipped into the liquor store and grabbed the Hennessey. "Yeah, aight. How he gonna look like me when she married that nigga? How you know it ain't his kid?"

"Because lil youngin' 'bout five or six. And if I recall, that's the same amount of years it's been since you first fucked Selena." He pointed a stiff finger into the center of Rasim's chest. "Do the math, homie." He stepped off and proceeded to the Funyuns aisle.

Rasim brushed him off because he knew it wasn't his kid. Selena said she had a child with her husband. He didn't want one but if he was a father, he would deal with it as best he could.

After buying the liquor, a large cup and a soda they were a block away from where they perched but before reaching Donald and Chance, Rasim said, "Hold this for a second." He gave him the bag.

Always the jokester, Rasim poured all of the Hennessey into the cup and then poured the soda into the Hennessey bottle. Since his gag required three-part harmony, he poured all of the Hennessey from the cup into the soda bottle.

"I can't believe you fucking up that nigga's bottle," Brooklyn said witnessing the ignorance.

"I ain't fucking it up," Rasim glowered. "It's in here." He raised the soda bottle.

"Yeah, but you got soda remnants mixed with his sauce and shit. You fucking up the flavor."

Rasim waved him off and tossed the cup away.

"Alright, but when Donald cave your chest cavity in, don't come crying to me."

The friends headed back to the pumping area and Rasim handed Donald the soda dressed in a Hennessey bottle just as Phantom's black Mercedes caressed the block.

Whenever he arrived, everybody, if they were fucking around, stopped. Everyone fell in line, along with Donald, Phantom was Rasim's other idol. When he parked he rolled down the window and looked at Donald. His five o'clock shadow sparkled like black diamonds. And the gold chain he donned fell against his black sweater.

He motioned with his head for Donald to come and Donald moved without hesitation.

Donald slipped inside of the Benz and melted into the black leather seat. And from the half rolled down window, Rasim and the fellas could see it all. It was as if they were watching an episode of *The Sopranos*.

As Donald got comfortable, Phantom observed the young hustler before saying a word. Although he was certain that Donald had enough gall, confidence and spirit necessary to run the block, he wanted to steal a few more moments to make sure he hadn't missed a thing. After he swept over him with prying eyes and was certain his decision to promote him was solid, he leaned back in his seat and the leather moaned. "What's in the bag?"

Donald pointed at it and said, "Oh this? The brown."

"You not gonna offer me a cup?"

Donald grinned and said, "Phantom, you can have anything you want. That's on my life."

Luckily for Donald, Phantom wasn't into niggas because he'd likely be on all fours with an ass full of dick after that declaration.

As Rasim stole peeks into the Benz in lieu of straight gawking he noticed how giddy Donald appeared. Around the crew, he was always serious and dark. What was different now? He guessed in the presence of a God he was fumbling. Rasim wanted the type of power that Phantom possessed for himself.

Prepared for everything, Phantom dipped into his oversize armrest and released two plastic cups.

That's when Rasim wanted to shit himself, knowing full well that he had the real Hennessey in the soda bottle in his hand.

"I've been observing you and decided to elevate your status," Phantom announced. "You're a hard worker and you're always on the block and I like that about you."

Neither had taken a sip of the soda yet and Rasim was grateful.

"But I'm gonna be watching how you operate too. It's one thing to lead your flock when you're on the same level. It's an entirely different thing to rule on high."

"I'm up for it," Donald said looking directly into his eyes. His right leg shook rapidly because he wanted this so badly his dick was beginning to stiffen. "You can count on me, Phantom. I'm as hard as they come."

Donald appreciated his vigor. "To prosperity," Phantom said as he raised his cup in the air in preparation for a toast.

"To prosperity," Donald responded in kind.

Their cups knocked together and the moment Phantom took a gulp he winced and spit into the cup. Then he rolled the window down further and tossed the cup out. "You gotta start drinking better shit, man."

Donald took a sip too and tasted the drink. He tasted the sweetness of the soda. He immediately peered over at Rasim who was covered in guilt. "Yeah, you're right," Donald said under his breath.

"Aight, well let me collect this money. You do what you do. I'll have Paul hit you up later with that pack." Phantom dapped him up and Donald slipped out of the car.

As Phantom's car vanished into thin air, Rasim was already preparing to cop a plea. "I'm sorry, man," Rasim said shaking his head as Donald approached. "I didn't know you were gonna share your shit with the boss."

"I told you this nigga play too much," Chance responded stuffing his hands in his jacket and shaking his head.

Instead of breaking his jaw like the old Donald would've, he embraced him and grabbed his other boys too. The four of them acted like excited football players who won the Super Bowl as opposed to the drug mongers they really were. They slapped each other on the backs and Donald even took to smooching Chance and Brooklyn's heads. Donald didn't have time to be mad. It was a celebration because he was essentially a made man.

After he separated from the herd, Donald looked at Rasim and jokingly said, "Now give me my drink before I really do break your jaw."

Rasim handed him the drink and tried to hide his excitement. He wondered how Donald felt now that he was in charge and he wanted nothing more than to be in his shoes.

The fellas were just coming down off of their high when trouble stepped on the block in the form of Levi, Terry and Wayne. They were knuckleheads from a rival project up the block and Donald hated them niggas. The most ironic part was that they were on foot when they could've been killed on the spot. Their fearless act was to display their bravery, not their foolishness.

Levi's story was straightforward. He used to own the very blocks Donald and his crew were pumping on but when he got locked up for a week, Donald swooped in and planted his flag and Levi had been salty ever since. That's one of the reasons Phantom fucked with him. He admired how he roughed his real estate.

When Donald saw them getting closer, he knew what time it was. "Brooklyn, give me the dragon," he said referring to his .45 tucked in the large bush a few feet over from where his crew rocked out.

Brooklyn quickly obeyed and Donald cocked it. Brooklyn grabbed his 9mm and handed Chance a revolver.

Now that the men were strapped, Donald looked back and saw Rasim who was hanging around frightened and unarmed. "Get out of here, Rasim! We'll get up with you later."

"You sure?" Rasim asked trying to sound noble.

"Bounce, nigga," Donald roared. "This shit ain't for you!"

Rasim was the funny man and neither Donald nor his other friends looked at him as anything different. Still, he felt bad leaving his boys but he also knew they were right. He was not a gangster so he left his soldiers on the battlefield and drove home.

☘☘ ☘☘

Rasim was standing in the middle of the floor pacing in circles. After he spoke to Donald and found out that the niggas who came on the block didn't want the heat and left without drama, he thought he would rest easy, go home and fuck Snow.

He was wrong.

His hand trembled as he held the phone to his ear. "Please help me," he said in a robust voice. "My life is on the line!"

"But I don't know where she is, Rasim," Maureen said truthfully. "The only thing she told me was that she had to get away."

"Did she leave a new number at least?" he asked with raised eyebrows. "Because she's not answering the phone."

"We are her parents, Rasim. Of course she gave us a way to contact her but I'm not at liberty to give it to you."

"Please, Mrs. Bradshaw," he begged with his voice hitting soprano notes. Before he came home, he had to piss but now his body had forgotten all about it. "I made a mistake but I don't deserve to have my girl taken over this shit. Please, I'm on my knees!"

"Son, I hear you and I know you love my daughter," she said with more compassion than she originally felt when he first called, "but Snow is a fragile angel. She's not meant for this world. She's meant for a man who can protect her and keep her heart safe and you failed. Which is sad because she always referred to you as Superman. I guess it was all a lie. Goodbye, Rasim. Be well."

Stupid old bitch!

Rasim threw his phone against the wall and it crashed and scattered to the floor. He dropped down, squatted and placed his hands over his face. His gut rolled and he felt like he was on the verge of throwing up.

There's nothing worse than losing somebody you thought would always be there and now Rasim understood true pain.

When he was fucking around with them bitches, he honestly thought that Snow would never depart. If he be-

BY T. STYLES

lieved that she would, he would have never overplayed his hand.

When he arrived home fully expecting to see her beautiful face, what he found was the empty side of her closet instead. After he kissed her kitty for hours straight the night before, he was certain that he'd done enough to reel her back in. Besides, she loved that shit. But Snow came to the conclusion that he wasn't a good guardian of her heart, so she took the key back and bounced.

The first day turned into a week. The weeks turned into a month and Rasim was still hopeful that Snow would return. He even visited her school only to learn that she withdrew.

He decided to pay Mute Candy a visit and of course it didn't end well. In her usual manner, she cursed him out but felt bad hours later when she remembered how hysterical he was. To repent, she went to his house and prepared enough food for Rasim to last a week and left. But her loyalty lay with Snow so that would be the extent of her help. She would not have done that but Snow took care of that man for over six years and she felt he needed a fair start.

Rasim couldn't accept how much time had passed without holding Snow and making love to her. He always said she was his heart but now he understood it physically.

Before long, two months turned into seven and Rasim lost so much weight he was almost unrecognizable. Since he was already slim, Rod from uptown accused Rasim of hitting the pipe. The trouble was word got back to Donald and he repaid Rod for the slight with two shiny black eyes.

Although broken, Rasim would appear on the block every day but do nothing but bring his homies down. It's a good thing Donald was in charge because he made certain that the crew picked up his slack. Nobody minded much. They all loved Rasim like a brother and they hated the pain he was in...again.

To make matters worse, he hadn't spoken to his father, who also refused to let him see his mother. He was really alone. So he wrote him a letter apologizing for not being the son he wanted him to be and begged him once more to not involve himself with Al-Qaeda. He also begged him to reach out to him. Kamran never responded.

It was seven o'clock a.m. on a Tuesday morning when his cell phone rang. His home phone was turned off so he didn't receive calls there. He reached for this phone, which was on the table next to the bed. "Hello," he said in a low voice.

"Hey, sexy. It's me. Selena."

Rasim frowned. "Choke on a bag of dicks, bitch," he said so calmly Selena wasn't sure she heard him correctly.

She wouldn't get a chance to ask either because he ended the call and tossed the bitch to the bed. Selena had single handedly caused him to lose Snow and he couldn't stand the sound of her name or her voice any longer.

As he lay in bed, he focused on the ceiling. One hand rested on his thin chest and the other behind his head. After so much time, he finally came to the realization that Snow was gone.

Possibly forever.

He had to pull himself together and move on with his life or else he would fall deeper into despair. Although he would never forget Snow, his heart told him that if they were meant to be, she would come back but only if the time was right.

Rasim eased out of bed, stepped over his clothes and the dirty dishes that littered the floor. He made plans to come back later that night and clean up his room and life.

When he was done he showered, slipped on his clothes and hopped in his car. As he drove down the road, he was amazed at the sapphire colored sky. Not a cloud was present and in a way it matched his mood...peaceful, relaxed and calm.

When he parked on the block, Rasim sidled out of his car and dapped Donald, Brooklyn and Chance before sitting on the step.

"This for you, man." Chance handed Rasim a cup of hot coffee.

Brooklyn tossed a white bag in Rasim's lap. "That's a glazed donut. We bought extras in case you wanted one and shit."

Rasim nodded in appreciation of his amigos and they noticed something different. His features were softer and not as distressed and it was obvious that he had gone through the worst stage of the storm.

Donald placed a firm hand on his shoulder and said, "Welcome back, homie."

With the sentiments of the heart out of the way, Donald decided to take the attention off his friend. "So Kelly was mad at me again today," he said referring to his wife.

"What you do this time?" Rasim asked, contributing to the conversation. It was the first time he uttered a word outside of *I need Snow* in months.

"You know how women are. I wasn't feeling good so she wanted to stay home from work to take care of me. I told her to go 'head because sick or not, I was hitting the block."

Brooklyn crossed his arms over his chest and jammed his hands under his armpits. "Hold up, you sick and you just shared a blunt with me a minute ago in the car?" he questioned, pointing at him.

"You ain't gonna die, nigga. You can't catch what I got anyway."

"You said that shit the last time and I had the flu for a month," Brooklyn continued. "It's real foul that I eat right but I still get sick fucking with you nasty ass niggas."

Rasim shook his head and peered up at Donald. He did seem ill but in his lovesick haze he never noticed before. "Do you know what's wrong, slim?"

Donald kicked at nothing on the ground. "The doctor trying to say it's cancer and shit but he can suck my dick."

Rasim, Chance and Brooklyn surveyed him with wide eyes. Donald acted as if he had a cold and now they discovered it was something fatal.

Concerned, Rasim sat his coffee and bag on the ground and approached him. "When were you gonna tell us that shit?"

Donald waved it off. "I'm telling ya'll now," he responded as he looked over their heads at more of nothing. He was trying to stall and get off of the subject. "And please don't start with me. I heard enough from my wife." Donald wiped his hand from his forehead to the back of his scalp. His hands dropped down and he decided to keep shit genuine. "I just keep thinking about my girls, you know?" He looked at Rasim and then the fellas. "If I die, what's gonna happen to them?"

"On my dick, your kids gonna be straight," Brooklyn said shooting from the heart. He could've worded it a bit differently but they were hood niggas who loved deep.

"I feel the same," Chance responded. "You'll never have to worry about shit in the way of them girls. Believe that."

Rasim stared directly into Donald's eyes. "You already know my heart. As long as I got breath in my body, your girls gonna be raised like they mine."

"Oh my God," Trina from across the street yelled, crashing the somber mood. "We under attack!"

Now, Trina was known to be a little over the top at times but something told Rasim that this situation was different. So he jogged across the street and put his hands softly on her shoulders as he gaped at her. "What's wrong with you?"

Trina's red face was sweaty and she appeared to be hyperventilating as she looked up at the icy blue sky. "Bombs just hit the World Trade Center in New York! We under attack!"

Suddenly a few older busybodies rushed outside of the building too. This was odd because they never emptied their apartments until it was time to unload a cheap bottle of vodka and discuss the latest scandal on the front step.

Yet there they were, embracing each other as they muttered what Trina had just said. That the United States was under attack.

When Rasim looked behind him he saw Donald, Chance and Brooklyn trot toward the elderly ladies. Rasim felt as if things were moving in slow motion and he couldn't hear a sound until Trina wiggled out of his grasp. He forgot that he was even holding her.

Rasim watched as the women said something to Donald to cause his face to distort. Whatever was communicated forced him backwards as he crashed to the ground like he missed his chair. Never down for long, he hopped

PRISON THRONE

up and sprinted toward his silver Infiniti, slid over the hood and jumped into the driver's seat.

Rasim rushed over to Brooklyn and Chance to get the word but both of them were holding their heads while their mouths hung open.

"What's wrong with Donald?" Rasim yelled.

Chance's eyes flapped a few times as if he were trying to wake up from a horrible dream. When Rasim rocked him roughly, Chance finally said, "The World Trade Center towers were hit by two planes. And the Pentagon too."

"So what's wrong with Donald?" Rasim asked, unable to follow how Donald was directly related. If they were at war, everyone was in trouble not just him.

"His wife works at the Pentagon, man," Brooklyn whispered.

Now it was clear.

Rasim whipped his head in the direction Donald moved. There was no way he was letting him drive alone in the frantic condition he was in. So he bolted across the street just as a DC Cab was speeding his way. Angry, Rasim slapped the hood once when it stopped, before he dipped toward the passenger seat of Donald's car.

Rasim slipped inside and at first Donald's eyes rolled around and he glared at him but Rasim didn't care. He was going with him whether he wanted to or not. "I'm riding, man," Rasim said as he watched tears roll down Donald's face. "I can't let you be out here by yourself."

Donald, who was always the big bad bear, broke down in tears as he jerked his car into traffic. He recited repeatedly that he couldn't lose his wife. That he would die without his family and be on some serial killer shit. Although Rasim was not married to Snow, he knew the pain of losing the one you loved.

When Rasim's keys fell to the floor and he bent down to retrieve them, Donald stopped suddenly and held Rasim's head down with a firm grip to the back of his neck. Rasim saw his life flash before his eyes.

Donald was about to kill him.

Seconds later, gunfire blasted into the car in all directions, moving the car with small thuds. Shards of glass bounced off the back of Rasim's neck as Donald's grip lessened.

Tires screeched and an engine revved up and Rasim knew what happened. His best friend was just murdered.

Slowly Rasim raised his head and Donald's hand slid off of him. Broken glass clinked as it poured off of his body and bounced against the floor. He looked out ahead of him, through the shattered windshield, afraid of facing Donald just yet.

Donald had pushed Rasim down to save his life and because of it, he still breathed. He was a real nigga to the end.

His neck muscles tensed as he forced himself to rotate his head in Donald's direction. It was more catastrophic than he thought. Rasim's hands shook as he saw the condition they left the homie in. His skull was blasted open, which exposed the frontal lobe of his brain. His face was shredded and not one of his features remained.

If he hadn't jumped inside of his car, he would've sworn the corpse to his left was not his man.

Heartbroken yet again, Rasim dragged his fingers down the sides of his face and howled.

PRISON THRONE

Rasim spent an hour at the hospital saying the same thing repeatedly to the officers. That he had no clue who killed Donald Guzman. Of course it was bullshit and the detectives knew it too. But it was a street matter and was not in their department.

Eventually the interrogation ceased.

During that time, Rasim learned that Donald's wife perished in the Pentagon attack. A large piece of debris struck her over the head, stealing her from her family in the process.

It was at that time that Rasim remembered that Donald's twin daughters would probably be alone. So he picked them up from school.

As he drove down the road, he glanced at them in the backseat. He was amazed that with all of the calamity happening around them, they were totally unaware. Their pink book bags sat in their laps and he asked himself, where would he take the children?

He went to Donald's parents' house and told them about their son and daughter-in-law's death. They were upset at the loss of their only child and shed two tears apiece. But they refused to accept their grandchildren. So with nothing left to do, he took them to his house.

After he made them hot dogs with no bread and French fries, he watched them play with their dolls on the sofa. He was delaying the inevitable. He had to tell the children that their parents were gone forever.

Rasim stuffed his hands into his pocket and looked down at Amber and Cassie with pity. He reduced his height and stood on his knees. At first they felt Uncle Rasim was being strange because he was silent and real close to them. They hoped he wouldn't try to touch their private parts that their father told them to protect. But after awhile, he told them how their lives would be changed.

They cried long and hard and wrapped their little arms around his neck. Rasim held them tightly, one in each bicep and kissed their wet cheeks. When he was done, he called the cousin of the one person he knew could help.

Mute Candy got there in thirty minutes flat. The moment she laid eyes on the girls, who were as sweet as sugar cane, she knew she would do whatever she could to help them. Mute Candy had a place of her own and no children inside so she didn't mind keeping them until they had a more suitable home. This made Rasim adore her even more.

He didn't bother asking about Snow because it was the wrong place and time. Instead, he jumped in his car and drove to his parents' house next.

Despite the terrorist attack, he wasn't concerned that his father was involved because he called his mother earlier in the day and, although clearly upset, she said Kamran didn't go and was at home. Apparently Kamran felt as if he betrayed his nation and Rasim felt worse when he discovered that it was due to the letter he had written.

Devastated, Rasim pulled up to the house and took a moment to slap the Kufi on his head. It seemed a bit ridiculous, all things considered, but it was a habit he couldn't break.

When he tried to enter his parents' house with the key, he was surprised to find it wasn't working. Kamran changed the locks shortly after he forbade Rasim to come over and it was the first time he tried.

He approached the window in the back of the house. Hoping to enter from the basement, he was shocked to see Umar on her knees next to her husband who was hunched over. She was weeping and Rasim was trying to figure out what was happening. So he pressed his face against the window and Rasim saw his father's head covered in blood.

What the fuck was going on?

His eyes widened and he banged on the window forcefully when he saw Umar pick up the gun that rested next to Kamran's head. She looked at the window, smiled and said I love you before placing the barrel to her temple and tugging the trigger.

There was no way she was living in this world without her dear husband. So she bid the universe a goodbye.

It seemed like everything was in slow motion as he banged on the window so hard it fractured against his blows and his hand bled. Everything he loved about life died in that moment.

And he could never be the same if he tried.

THE NEXT DAY

Rasim stood in front of the mirror without a shirt. His body was scrawnier than it was before. You could clearly see his skeleton beneath his skin. With the death of his father and mother yesterday, he was starting to hate the people of his country even more. He blamed them for his father's suicide and he hadn't gotten a moment's sleep.

As he reviewed his reflection in the mirror, he raised the large gray rock in his hand. Gripping it tightly, he slammed it against his right eye. The pain rippled from the front of his head and rushed to the back but he wasn't done.

Blood sprayed from his upper and lower eyelid and splashed against the mirror. He slammed the rock into his head so many times his face was crimson.

Trying to dissociate himself from his own people, he was hoping to alter his appearance.

Before long, he felt lightheaded due to losing so much blood and he plummeted to the floor.

CHAPTER 12

SNOW

When Snow walked into the home she used to share with Rasim, she was about to leave back out, believing she entered the wrong place. Instead she paused at the doorway and glanced at the jumble. It was a complete disaster but even that would be an understatement. Clothes, dirty dishes and trash littered the floor and it was possessed by the rank odor of decaying food.

What was Rasim doing with his life?

What was he thinking?

When Snow bounced on him months earlier, she never meant for him to tumble so hard in her absence. She didn't even do it on purpose. She just made a decision that she would no longer allow him to hurt her feelings and dipped.

Whether he knew it or not, he succeeded in breaking her down so well that it hurt more to be with him than without him. She quickly made moves to allow for her new resolve too, which was why she also dropped out of school.

The last thing she needed was to be dancing her heart out only for Rasim to show up begging. She would've relented. She was certain. And this time had to be different. So she continued dancing at her new place.

The moment she left, after he licked her clean and hit the block, she didn't even bother to shower. Instead she rose from that pissy smelling floor, grabbed her clothes and moved on.

As the days smoothed by, she developed a pocket of hate on the left side of her heart. She used it as fuel to advance each day without him. If he wanted Selena, they could have each other. After awhile, although she still loved him and thought of him a lot, she learned that she could live without him.

And then 9/11 happened.

When Snow met up with her best friend after the tragedy facing their nation, she was surprised to see her with Donald's twins. Mute Candy tried to act normal, as if she got them all the time but Snow was no longer naive. So Mute Candy was forced to tell her the entire ordeal. How Donald was murdered in front of Rasim. How she got word from Brooklyn and Chance that Rasim's parents were killed the same day. Snow knew that but for the sake of God, who Rasim did not respect, he would die without her help.

Snow was many things but a brute was not one of them. She could never abandon Rasim in his hour of need and she decided that it was time to reach out and pull him from the bowels of hell. If not, he would be lost forever.

Taking a deep breath first, she tossed her purse in the area that used to be the sofa and the mess swallowed it whole. From where she stood, she couldn't see the strap of her Gucci anymore.

"Rasim," she whispered stepping over the rubbish. "Rasim, where are you?" Her footsteps were short and deliberate and if she was being honest, she was petrified.

Although she wanted to hear him respond, something felt off. Her sixth sense was activated and she knew something dark was brewing in the home that was once brimming with love. It felt like an evil spirit, or a man who was so distressed that he no longer maintained custody of his soul. Both were equally dangerous.

With bravery on her side, Snow bent corner after corner until she happened upon the bathroom. What she saw next caused her heart to stutter. Her eyes spread and she gripped at the doorframe to prevent from crashing down.

Rasim, her precious Rasim, was lying on the bathroom floor, halfway under the sink with blood pouring out of the gash on his face.

"Oh my God, what have you done?" she proclaimed clutching her chest.

Pure panic snatched her body and she descended to her knees. Suddenly she realized that although she was there to help Rasim, if this man was dead, who on God's green planet would save her?

Slowly she crawled toward him, creating a trail of blood in the process. Huge tears trickled down her face and splashed against the floor. When she finally reached him, she gripped him with all of her strength and placed his head into the center of her lap. Tear after tear slapped against his face as she caressed his bloodied cheek.

With him in her arms, she glanced over at the red rock.

What had he done to his beautiful face?

Why had he altered what was always perfect in her eyes?

"Rasim," she said in a squeaky voice. "Oh my God, Rasim, please talk to me, baby. Please don't do this shit unless you want me to die too. I'm begging you! Have mercy on me. Don't fucking leave me! Not like this!"

BY T. STYLES

Although she pleaded, he still wouldn't open his eyes.

And then it happened. A movement so slight that at first she thought her mind was playing games. She leaned closer to his face and then she was certain. Rasim Nami was attempting to open his left eye. He would've attempted to do both but the right was pasted shut with coagulated blood.

When he finally looked up at his angel, he thought he was dreaming. Figuring it would only be in death that he would meet her again, he asked, "Am I dead?"

She shook her head rapidly. Her face was so red it looked as if she were holding her breath. A vein she never knew existed protruded down the middle of her forehead and pulsed. "You're alive, baby. You're alive!"

Rasim rose up and wrapped his arms around Snow's neck. He held her so tight Snow could barely breathe. The smell from his underarms wafted in the air and resembled the odor of bad marijuana. But Snow didn't care. He was her man.

He was her Rasim.

"I'm so sorry, baby," he declared, doing all he could to prevent from crying. "I'm so fucking sorry for hurting you and I will never do it again, Snow. Thank you for coming back to me. Thank you so much."

Snow wanted to rejoice too but she heard it all before. He would make promises as high as the moon that graced the sky. As high as the heavens where she believed God roamed. And when it was all said and done, in the end, he would hurt her again.

"I can't take it anymore, Rasim," she wept gripping him tightly as her nose nestled in the pit of his neck. She was astonished at how her arms were able to wrap around his body due to him losing so much weight. "If you hurt me again, I'll be forced to attack. You would leave me no other choice."

"I know," he said holding the back of her head as he continued to hug her. His blood smeared against the side of her face. "I know." He kissed her ear repeatedly because it was the first place he could reach.

"I love you, Rasim," she proclaimed. "I love you so fucking much and all I'm asking is that you love me back. Is that too much?"

He placed his lips against her ear so that she could feel each word with the intensity of thunder. "Snow, I will put a bullet in my head before I hurt you again. I'm ready. I'm ready to fight for you. I'm ready to tell these bitches to kick rocks and protect our home. So much shit has happened in my life. But with you in my corner," he thought about Donald and his parents and felt himself on the verge of crying so he paused, "but with you in my life, baby, I got a chance."

And it was just like that.

Just like it was in the Strawberry Meadows days, if we're being honest.

Snow Bradshaw, Rasim's God sent angel, had made the decision to save his life.

Again.

So she eased on her feet and helped Rasim to the bedroom. She pushed piles of junk off the bed and sat him on the edge of it as if he were a stiff doll. She tended to his wound, placing gauze over his eye and wrapping an Ace bandage around his head to stop the bleeding. Now that he was safe, she whipped around their bedroom like the Tasmanian Devil cartoon character until all of the dirty clothing sat in white, colored and dark piles in the middle of the floor.

When she was done with that, she asked him to rest on a chair in the room against the wall while she placed new sheets that Rasim didn't even know he owned on the bed. The man didn't know shit. He didn't take care of himself when she left and became a wreck.

When the sheets were changed, she took a bar of soap and a washcloth and grabbed a bucket and filled it with warm water. Standing in their bedroom, she removed his clothes and wiped his body down. The tub was too filthy to bathe him in so that would have to do.

Rasim wanted to weep as he looked down at her but she hadn't given him a moment's stare. She was on a mission to get him back in order. Loving Rasim properly was serious work.

Once he was clean, she tucked him in the bed, which smelled of fresh jasmine, and zipped out of the house to go to the store.

Since the house was in a horrible way, of course she had to call in reinforcements. And who better to save the day than her best good girlfriend Mute Candy?

Like a loyal soldier, Mute Candy stepped up without a moment's delay. First she asked her favorite cousin to watch Donald's girls and when Snow and Mute Candy returned from the store they cleaned the living room, bathroom and hallways from top to bottom, just like they did in the Strawberry Meadows days.

When the house was immaculate, they washed each piece of clothing and Mute Candy went into the kitchen to prepare a meal for Snow's king.

Rasim low key preferred Mute Candy's chicken to Snow's anyway but she'd never let Snow know. The funniest thing is she didn't have to. Snow knew everything about her man, including his love for her best friend's chicken and it didn't bother her in the least.

As long as he was happy, as long as he was safe, Snow was good.

While dinner was being prepped, Snow ran a tub full of warm water and helped Rasim inside. Now she could properly wash his troubles away. As she dipped the washcloth into the warm water and squeezed it over his skin, she could feel the demons trying to maintain power over his body.

She wanted them gone.

She wanted them away.

For this man did not belong to them.

The pain over losing his parents and best friend was written all over his face. So she placed her warm hand over his heart. "Let it out, Rasim," she whispered in a compassionate tone. "Don't be afraid to cry in front of me. I will never judge you."

Rasim wanted to release so badly his dick was hardening but not in front of Snow. He had to be strong. He had to save face. Besides, he didn't want his woman, his love, looking at him in a pitiful way.

Instead his cheek bubbled on the left side of his face just like his father's did the last time he saw him and he held back his tears from Rasim. Instead he sucked his troubles back in just as Kamran had done before he died. The problem was Rasim forgot what not releasing could do to a man's soul in the long run, but for now Snow would let it ride.

She carefully removed the bandage from Rasim's head and wiped the blood off of his face, revealing the true condition of the wound on his eye. She pleaded on bended knees for him to go to the hospital but he refused. He would allow the gash to heal as it wanted, thereby being a constant reminder of the worst day of his life.

When he was loved up, clean and dry she moistened his skin with lotion. Of course she planted soft kisses over his body in the process but that was for free. That only occurred when the love in her heart was so strong that it boiled over to the surface and she had to kiss him because she couldn't take it anymore.

With each kiss, he was recharged although when his battery was filled, he would be different from the man she fell in love with. This man, a much stronger one, no doubt, would love harder but to the world he would be both cold and hard.

After he was dressed, Snow escorted Rasim to the kitchen where he sat at the head of the table. Mute Candy placed a plate of food in front of him, bent down, kissed him on his left cheek and went back to work. She wanted him to know that she loved him and that she was truly happy that he was back in her best friend's life.

When there was a soft knock at the door, Snow opened it. Chance and Brooklyn eased inside with somber looks on their faces. Snow called them earlier because she knew they were just as worried about their best friend as she was.

Rasim wasn't some nigga they kicked it with when the mood or the money was right. He was their brother and they loved him harder than a can of old paint.

Before addressing Rasim, Brooklyn pulled Snow into a strong hug, kissed her on the cheek and said, "Thank you for saving my man's life. Again. I love you."

She softly touched the side of his face and said, "I love you too."

PRISON THRONE

When Brooklyn walked around her to check on the welfare of his brother, Chance embraced Snow just as strongly. He also kissed her on the head and she touched him on the face.

When they were finished properly greeting the queen, they walked over to the table to confer with the king. The moment they saw Rasim's face, the three men enclasped one another as they fought back tears that were rightfully theirs due to the loss of Donald, due to the loss of Rasim's parents and due to the state of their country.

When they were done, Snow fed the other two men and Mute Candy grabbed plates for herself, the girls and her cousin. Since her work was done, she bid them farewell and left them alone.

After getting her plate, Snow retreated to the living room like she did in the Strawberry Meadows days. With her love being implanted in Rasim's heart, she knew a real man also needed the connection of his comrades to properly heal.

But when she saw Rasim's cup was empty she sat her plate on the sofa, hopped up and refilled his juice before doing the same for the fellas.

Back in the day, Chance and Brooklyn thought her behavior was weird but boy did they feel stupid now. They realized that their friend had been blessed with what both of them would kill for. A bitch that embodied the epitome of what it meant to truly hold a nigga down.

When they were done, they left and Snow cleaned up the kitchen and escorted her man to the bed. But she was about her shit. Her work was far from over.

So she showered and covered her damp skin in Rasim's favorite Chanel body lotion but that was about it. Why bother putting on clothes when they were such frivolous things? Instead, as naked as the day she last fucked him, she slipped into the bed. And yes…Rasim was waiting.

Crouched over top of him like the sun, she lowered her head and placed tiny kisses on his big toes before gracefully moving to his ankles, covering his legs with lip caresses until she somehow found herself on top of his dick.

Rasim was so aroused that he was rock hard and oozing with pre-cum.

His bitch was back!

All hail Snow!

The one woman who was made for him. The woman who was designed in his image had proven why her heart should not have been toyed with in the first and second place.

She was strong. She meant what she said and he realized that although Snow loved him, she would not hesitate to disappear if he didn't honor their agreement and broke her heart again.

My, my, my, had Snow changed.

Her fuck game was spectacular. Worthy of an award with the prestige of an Oscar.

Snow felt her man trembling like an old car starting up on a cold day. But she wanted to taste him. She wanted his sweet cream down her throat. So she eased up and provided his dick shelter within the walls of her mouth.

Rasim moaned louder than he ever knew was possible. Her tongue circled and traced the base of his stick but he held back. Why was he holding back?

It was time for a conversation.

For if they were going to fuck, then he had better act like it.

So she stopped and looked up at him. "Rasim, I belong to you," she glared. "You can't hurt me if you tried. Now stop treating me delicately and fuck me like you know it."

Shit. Why didn't she say that at first?

He palmed her head like a hood nigga who was nice with the basketball and fucked her throat as if he were collecting points. Snow didn't gag once because when they were together he taught her how he liked to be sucked so her throat was relaxed.

She was cool on holding her breath. She could worry about breathing later. Right now it was all about Rasim.

And for her dedication, she was rewarded with a trail of cream down her esophagus.

Poor Rasim.

He couldn't handle Snow's new and improved fuck game if he tried. All he wanted was to go to sleep but it was too early. And the whole thing about it was that she was far from done. She crawled on top of him, dripping wet pussy and all. Snow hit the switches on that nigga like a tricked out ride in Cali.

In awe, he gripped at her hips as he felt himself heavy with the desire to cum again. So he did and his semen pushed out of his body as he hollered so loudly and strong that he gave himself a sore throat.

It was the best sex he ever had.

In his life.

Nobody had shit on Snow and that went for freaky Selena too.

Now that her work was done, Snow ran her hands through her damp hair and her titties bounced like paddleballs. It was her time to get off.

"I swear to God you made for me," he moaned. He looked upon her in amazement.

Snow heard him, no doubt, but Rasim was preaching to the choir. In full fuck mode, she rode that nigga so strong and so hard that at the end of the night, he asked her to be his wife.

On Monday, October 1, 2001, Rasim and Snow became husband and wife.

Although they were newlyweds, they were married in an uneventful ceremony. Snow wasn't interested in a big to do. All she wanted was to be what she always desired... his wife.

After they were joined by the ring, they had a small gathering at their house and Mute Candy, Donald's daughters, Brooklyn and Chance came over to celebrate. Snow's parents dropped by too and they were happy for the young couple because, if nothing else, the Bradshaws knew that their love was pure. Even if it didn't work.

The next day it was honeymoon time. Snow located an all-inclusive resort and they were scheduled to see Jamaica, a place neither of them ventured before.

But something was going on with Rasim that alarmed Snow. It was subtle but she saw it. When she met him in the beginning, he had joy in his heart and laughed and joked a lot. But since she returned to him, he didn't chuckle once.

She didn't take it personally. It was evident how much he adored her by the intensity he used when he gripped her as she stood at his side, as if he were protecting her from the elements of the world. His grief had nothing to do with Snow. He had simply lost his happiness for the rest of his life.

Snow did all she could to persuade him to open up and laugh again but nothing worked. She knew his heart was in pieces from his multiple losses but he refused to speak about those things.

As always, Snow was wise and she would not push him. It was her job to feed and clothe him, so that he would be safe.

Rasim and Snow were at the airport in the line preparing to go through the screening process. As they made their way to the front, people eyed the young couple suspiciously and both figured Rasim's half open right eye was the attention grabber. But as they continued down the line the stares grew stronger and more intense. Snow wondered what could be wrong?

When they reached the screener, a white man in his mid-thirties sat back in the chair with exaggerated casualness. "Identification please," he snapped at Rasim.

Rasim quickly handed him his passport. The screener investigated the document looking up at him every so often in the process. It was as if he were reading his dirty diary and learned horrible secrets about him.

"Rasim Nami, huh?" he said in a condescending tone. "What nationality is that?"

"Excuse me, sir?" He leaned in.

"I said what nationality?"

"I'm American," Rasim said proudly as his chest grew swollen with pride. He loved this country and he didn't want the screener thinking he had anything to do with the madness that occurred in New York, DC and

Pennsylvania or that he stood by the perpetrators, for that matter.

"I'm asking you what is your ethnicity," the screener shot back, now drawing a crowd. "Not where you were born!"

When Snow turned around and observed the expressions of the people in the line, it was evident that they enjoyed what was occurring. As if injuring her husband's feelings would bring back the thousands of people who died in the tragedy. What shocked Snow even more was that a few black people had the nerve to turn up their noses when they knew what their people had been through.

Snow was confused.

Why all the hate for a man who adored America?

Rasim swallowed and wiped the sweat that was brewing on his brow. "Sir, I am...Pakistani," he said under his breath. "But I was born in America."

The screener's brow lowered and he frowned. It was as if he wanted Rasim to lie about his background since he so-called loved America so fucking much. With a stiff finger, he pointed to his right. "Stand over there!"

"Is something wrong?" Rasim asked.

"Either stand over there or you won't get on that plane," he yelled. "Now move! There are other customers waiting."

Rasim and Snow trudged toward the section delegated not too far from the screener. For twenty minutes they endured cold glares from people as they looked upon Rasim with hate.

It was madness. Why were they angry with him? When those planes attacked, Rasim hurt too. And so did she. Couldn't they see? Why had they so quickly formed opinions based solely on his skin tone?

PRISON THRONE

When two security officers approached, one large African American male and a scraggy white male with a spotted face, Snow reasoned that things weren't going to get any better.

The men escorted both of them into a room off of the gate and bombarded Rasim with question after question. They wanted to know who he was and where he was going. What had he done before coming to the airport and what were his plans thereafter. They even hinted to wanting to know the relationship he had with Snow. What was next? Demanding to know how he fucked his new wife? If it was proper-like?

Although Snow was forced into the room as well, it was obvious that she was just guilty by association. Their real intended prey was Rasim Nami, her loving husband. She felt helpless as she watched them berate him simply because of his heritage.

To make matters worse, they made him take off his shirt and ran a wand up and down his bare skin. What did they think? That he had a bomb within his chest cavity? The white man produced a pair of latex gloves and put them on his hands. He looked over at a bottle of lubricant and considered using it to perform a thorough investigation.

Rasim looked over at Snow, feeling less than a man. With a heart heavier than a brick. He wasn't fit to be her husband. He couldn't even love her in public.

So he lowered his eyes and his body hunched over as his manhood was stomped on for their amusement and pleasure. All he wanted was to take his beautiful wife to an island and he feared that the trip would not happen.

When she saw a single tear hung in the corner of his eye, Snow's gut rolled. She didn't want the men to reap the benefits of their harsh behavior by seeing him broke down. For all she cared they could take the island of Jamaica and push it up their funky asses.

In the past Snow chose the soft-spoken route but boy was she tired of that shit. She was tired of biting her tongue and tired of not speaking her mind. In anger she yelled, "You two mothafuckas have taken enough of my husband's time."

Snow's intensity shocked Rasim and made him proud. Suddenly he was given the vigor he needed to be stronger.

The black officer's cheeks jiggled because Snow's spirit was so quiet a moment ago that he forgot she was even in the room. Who knew the walls could talk? Her voice possessed so much power. The white officer was just as shocked and his pockmarked skin turned a brilliant shade of blue.

"Baby, put your clothes on," Snow ordered feeling more empowered. "If they don't want us on their plane they can take it out back and fuck it! We out of here!"

Mr. and Mrs. Rasim Nami did not go out of town for their honeymoon and it wasn't the last time people held him personally responsible for the 9/11 attacks with their ugly stares and sly remarks.

Even the FBI took jabs by coming to the house asking Rasim a million questions about his parents and the organization that he knew nothing of.

Before long, Rasim's already hardened heart grew solid and only Snow possessed the recipe to make it soften.

PRISON THRONE

In order to relieve stress, Rasim took to bodybuilding. He grew stronger and bigger and never spoke about the 9/11 attacks or the loss of his people again. Even though there were more Americans who didn't hold Rasim accountable for what happened in the country, for some odd reason, he could only remember the faces of the many who did.

Things were bad but the devil made them worse the day Rasim received a frantic call from Chance. "You gotta come to the block, man! The nigga Levi set up shop and bragging to niggas that he killed Donald."

Rage.

Strong, unfettered rage, gripped Rasim's heart like a migraine headache. "Meet me at the liquor store," Rasim responded, breathing slowly through his nostrils. "I'm on my way."

From the kitchen, Snow heard the phone call and she could see the word "revenge" bling in both of Rasim's eyes. He wanted somebody to pay for his parents' suicide. He wanted somebody to pay for the racism he experienced as of late. And lastly he wanted the nigga responsible for Donald's death to glisten in his own blood.

When Rasim hung up the phone he moved with the gait of a zombie to the bathroom. His body was tense as he stepped in front of the mirror.

From the opened doorway Snow witnessed Rasim eyeing himself as he transformed to something dark and sinister in the mirror.

Rasim removed the Kufi from his pocket and pressed it on his head. If they wanted to make him a monster for being Pakistani and Muslim, then he would feed on their fear and turn it into power. He observed his right eye, which was permanently closed in the corner. He observed his body, which was free of flaws and tattoos. He didn't look like he felt inside but soon all that would change.

He knew what needed to be done and he was about to exit the bathroom when Snow stood in front of him. She knew what he was about to do; it was written all over his body as if she were reading a newspaper.

Her dear husband, her beautiful Rasim, was about to commit cold-blooded murder.

Rasim looked down at her, hoping that she wouldn't ask him to do something he couldn't...deny his friends help. Instead she touched the side of his face and said, "When you kill the nigga, make sure you're sick with it."

That was all that needed to be said.

When Rasim pulled up at the liquor store, Brooklyn and Chance were already standing out front with their hands stuffed in their jean pockets. Worry covered their faces as they paced the ground before them. It was cool though, Rasim held enough strength for the both of them.

Rasim hopped out of the car draped in an all black hoodie. The white Kufi on his head stood out for several reasons. For one, they never saw him wear it and for two, the contrast between the black and the white was so strong, a cop could see him from miles away. But he didn't give a fuck. It wasn't coming off.

"Where he at?" Rasim interrogated as he approached his brothers.

Both Brooklyn and Chance were taken aback by Rasim's stance. The jokester kid had vanished and in his place stood the man who whispered warrior.

Rasim was about that life.

"In front of the building," Brooklyn said trying to appear as hard as Rasim.

"Who over there with him?"

"His crew," Chance said. "The same 'ole hating ass niggas."

Rasim reached behind him and touched the handle of his gun.

"What you gonna do?" Brooklyn asked. Rasim didn't rock in this arena.

"Stay right here," he said seriously. "I'm gonna handle it."

"Naw, man, we called you for backup in case we need Phantom, but we got it," Chance said as he touched Rasim's arm.

When Rasim looked down at him as if he had violated and butt fucked his wife, Chance removed his hand.

"I said I'll handle it."

And that's exactly what he did.

Rasim didn't hop in his ride, roll down the window and blast Levi where he stood like in so many dope boy movies. He didn't hide in a corner of his apartment, jump out and shoot him either.

As cool as a fall evening, as cool as a summer rain, Rasim Nami walked methodically toward Levi as he stood on the block. In the same place he and Donald used to pump every day.

When Rasim got within a stone's throw of the niggas, he pulled his weapon, tugged the trigger and pierced

Levi's beating heart. Eyes open, Levi gripped his chest and fell to the ground.

The nigga was over.

Ironically, had it been Brooklyn or Chance, Levi and his boys would not have been so lackadaisical. In fact, they would've reached for their hammers and cut them down where they stood. But the gunman was Rasim, the funny kid of Pakistani descent. What could he possibly do to them?

Now it was too late. In an attempt to save their own lives, Levi's friends bolted up the street and Washington, DC had made it known that a new killer was born.

Terry took one look back, not believing it was him and continued his sprint home.

In full killer mode, Rasim stood over Levi's corpse with the barrel stretched as if it were an extension of his body and placed a hot spot ever so lightly in the middle of his forehead.

Aw. That's just right.

When he was done he removed his switchblade and gave Levi a Glasgow smile. It was a shoddy job, no doubt, but he would get better with time.

When his work was done, and only when it was done, he wiped his knife on Levi's shirt and slid off as smoothly as oil on a stiff dick.

PARTTHREE

BY T. STYLES

CHAPTER 13

RASIM

MAY 2012

Rasim Nami, acclaimed drug lord, sat in a wooden chair large enough to hold his naked muscular frame with Snow Nami in his lap. His chiseled biceps and torso were completely tatted and his most prized work of art, Snow's name, was etched across his heart with an iron gate in front of it. It symbolized not only that Rasim was a married man but also that he would protect her.

Snow was on top of her man as she rode his dick with an equestrian-like flow. Although Snow's body art paled in comparison to her husband's, she dabbled a little and as a result the entire right side of her body was covered, with the largest tat being Rasim's name, which appeared to crawl down her right thigh.

Rasim looked directly into Snow's eyes as he moved inside of her slowly. His left hand gripped the back of her neck and his right rested firmly on her waist. As good as her pussy was in the moment, if she moved one inch he was liable to kill her.

But Snow was inspired to switch shit up so she migrated from horse rider and embraced the passion of a young Jamaican dancer as she handled her beau with long smooth strokes.

Sweat poured down their faces as they were brought closer to ecstasy. Since they were covered in tats, they resembled two Jean-Michel Basquiat paintings straight fucking.

They didn't make a sound as they enjoyed each other's bodies. He looked upon her as Julius Caesar did Cleopatra. And she envisioned the Greek God Zeus when she gazed into his eyes.

Rasim was enamored and captivated and at times his love was so strong that he wished he could kill her then restore her life, just to fall in love all over again.

When Snow felt his dick pulsating she knew he was on the verge of exploding so she placed her hands on the edge of the chair against his thighs like a gymnast. Using her arm muscles she rose up and then slammed back on his stiffness five times and he could do nothing but tap out as he came hard.

After all these years my wife can still fuck, he thought.

Of course Snow saw the admiration Rasim felt for her. She had grown too over the years. No longer was she the mousy type who chose to speak few words.

When Rasim went through the storm after the loss of his best friend and his parents, he needed a strong woman at his side. So little by little, he created a bitch in his likeness. A woman who could deal with whatever came her way and he was proud of his accomplishment.

After making love, they jumped into the shower and embraced while kissing deeply. The showerhead dangled over their heads and the water poured over their bodies, bringing their tattoos to life.

BY T. STYLES

They were the couple people dreamed about. And they were all about each other.

When they were done Rasim got dressed and Snow wore only red pumps. She strutted to the kitchen and worked the stove like she was a DJ on the Ones and Twos. In the end, Rasim had a man's breakfast before him, complete with two kinds of meat, grits, potatoes and toast.

A lot changed about Rasim and Snow. Although they were still husband and wife, they were physically stronger. Rasim's body was chiseled and Snow's was firm and sleek. Their living arrangements also received a makeover. Rasim moved into his parents' home and renovated it into a castle and Snow was very pleased.

When Rasim was fed, Snow got dressed and hit it to The University of Baltimore Dance Academy to teach dance and he headed to the warehouse to move dope. Their paths were different but it was their life and they liked it that way.

The saddest part was that the more things stayed regular, the more things started to change.

The sun beamed down on Rasim's black Cadillac Escalade, causing it to glow. He gripped the steering wheel with his right hand and leaned slightly to the left. It wasn't because he was stunting. Rasim was already smooth. It's just that when your dick was as big as his, tilting a little made you slightly more comfortable.

As he cruised down the DC streets, the soft cotton gray shirt he wore melted into his frame causing the outlines of his muscles to be seen by all who chose to glance.

And because the window was open, the expensive cologne he sported whirled throughout the truck and mixed with the black ice car freshener that was hidden below his steering column.

A photographer at heart, he even snapped a few pictures for his personal collection although he would never get them developed.

At the end of the day even in a plain t-shirt and designer blue jeans, Rasim was mighty fresh.

His left hand rested next to his dick as he observed the sights and sounds of the city. Women wearing clothing so tight you could see the veins under their skin and the print of their pussies, squirmed up and down the blocks.

There was no doubt that the sexy vixens held his attention but unfortunately he could do nothing with them. For as much as he desired, he made a promise to remain faithful, which was growing harder to keep. Still, true to their agreement Rasim hadn't touched another woman since the last time he saw Selena. Almost eleven years ago.

There were many reasons for his faithfulness. Number one, he knew that no matter whom he dicked down, he would never leave Snow. He worshipped her so much that on several occasions he ate her pussy even while she was on her menstrual cycle.

The women whom he ran into in his travels flirted with him religiously but they didn't want to possess his body. They wanted Snow's career as his wife and that position was already taken.

The second reason for his faithfulness was that he believed Snow when she said if he ever fucked her over again that she would bounce. Although she held a fragile heart, she was the strongest woman he knew. She showed him when she left many years ago that she had the capacity to remain true to her word and it took the death of his parents and his best friend just to bring her back to him.

The third reason he couldn't cheat was because he upheld one rule that he used both in business and in life. And it was to never deal with a person who had nothing to lose.

Meeting a woman who had investments of the heart and business on the line was as uncommon as finding a DC nigga breaking bread with a Baltimore dude…it just didn't occur. If only the realization that he could only partake of Snow's pussy for the rest of his life would sit well with him, he would be fine. But as of now, he was severely bored.

Oh how he wished Snow would understand that he desired variety. If he dabbled in a new pussy here, and a new pussy there, it didn't mean that he didn't love her. Rasim was an alpha male! A king of kings! And as a result his sexual appetite craved more. Couldn't she see that?

It was different for men. It was a scientific fact, to hear him tell it.

No matter who he bent back, no matter who he had clawing the walls and screaming his name, his heart would always belong to her.

When he made it to the block and he saw Tracy, with the 3D ass, he gripped his thick dick and yelled, "Fuck!" That bitch was getting finer with time and he could only envisage about what she felt like inside.

Summertime was always toughest on Rasim but he would have to do like he always did. Go home with the impressions of sexy women on his mind and fuck the dog shit out of Snow for denying him a platter of assorted pussy.

As Rasim promenaded down the street he saw kids bouncing balls, niggas talking shit as they sipped from the brown paper bags clutched in their hands and women prattling with their backs toward the streets in the hopes of roping an up and coming dope star. However, the moment his trucked spooned the curb, the block died.

Rasim slinked out of his truck, pointed his remote at his ride and activated the security system. It chirped and he dropped the keys into his pocket. As cool as a Corona on ice, he gripped his dick slightly to reposition it and then released.

As he moved away from his Cadillac, he took a huge step, which nailed the sidewalk.

Now the block had life.

In his usual chill manner, Rasim advanced toward the building. He stroked the Kufi once as if he was smoothing his waves and nodded at a few people he knew. Although he didn't practice the Muslim beliefs, he wore it every day to warn those with dishonorable intents to beware. All who were around in the earlier years knew that before he wore that headpiece, he was a different man, a kinder gent. But these days, simply put, he was a stone cold killer.

There was something else about Rasim besides his strikingly good looks and features. He had a rock star quality that was undeniable and appealing. He was a far cry from the scrawny kid who joked around in the Strawberry Meadows days. That's for sure.

His presence was so alluring that children leveled their fingers in his direction as huge smiles consumed their faces. Batman didn't have shit on him. And lesser men in both the mental and dick departments even looked away for they were not worthy.

As the un-American idol continued to trek toward the building, if you looked closely you could see the ground shatter each time his butter colored Timberland boots slammed against the pavement.

When a little boy who promised to get better grades saw him moving in his direction, he caught wheels and leaped into his arms. Rasim hoisted the musty little fellow up on his broad shoulder and steadied his body with one hand as he reached into his pocket with the other. "What's up, lil man? You got that report card on you?"

Did he have it on him?

Hell yeah he did!

The lad carried it everywhere he went after receiving better grades in the hopes of seeing Rasim. Besides, Rasim promised him a crispy fifty-dollar bill if his shit was in order and in the little dude's mind, the moment he saw that truck, it was payday.

The kid pulled out the wrinkled report card, wet with the sweat of the day, and showed Rasim his progress.

Rasim considered it for a moment, saw the A's versus the D's and slapped a brand new one hundred dollar bill in his palm. The child's eyes grew as wide as saucers as he wiggled with excitement. And to think, it wasn't even his birthday.

Rasim placed the kid down although he took a moment to grip at his leg and said, "Thank you, Mr. Rasim! Thank you so much!"

When the kid bounced, Dee-Dee and Monique started twerking their young asses up and down in the hopes that Rasim was disbursing cash to everybody today. Unfortunately for the cuties, the Bank of Rasim was officially closed.

PRISON THRONE

When he finally approached the door leading into a large brick building, the two men protecting it, Erick and Fish, nodded and allowed him entrance. Before going inside, Rasim whispered something of major importance into Fish's ear that he wanted only him to hear. Once the intel was received, Fish nodded like the loyal soldier he was and Rasim swaggered inside.

He dipped sideways down the dark steps until he was looking at one of his soldiers spread on a silver table under a bright surveillance light. Sadly, it was Navy. His light skin was bruised, which indicated that he took a severe beating. There was no need for violins, however, because the shit was all his fault.

Two weeks ago Navy hired a new soldier named Detroit without properly vetting him to figure out his background. After not even two weeks, it was discovered that Detroit was working for the FBI. He was uncovered when Chance determined that he didn't like the way his plain white t-shirt bubbled ever so slightly in the front. So he ordered a silent pat down and voila! The wire was found.

Rasim's men spent an hour putting Detroit through unbearable torture after disarming the mic of course. In the end they found out that nine of Navy's men, including Detroit, were helping the government. But Vance was still on the run.

With the new info, they decided to handle Detroit first. After they operated on him with hammers and scalpels, they quietly dismembered his body parts and drove along the eastern coastline feeding the fish his limbs in the process.

With Detroit out of the way, along with all seven of his dwarfs, Rasim only had to care for Navy who was on his table and Vance who was effectively missing in action.

BY T. STYLES

On to the first order of business, Rasim dapped Chance and Brooklyn who had been waiting for his arrival. "Did ya'll find Vance?" Rasim asked.

Chance jabbed a stiff finger in the cup of Navy's throat. "Naw, this nigga claim he don't know where he at."

Navy looked upon Rasim with sorrow. "Rasim, I'm begging you, please don't kill me. If I knew where the nigga was I would've told you myself. Handed him to you with my own hands if you gave me a wheelbarrow. I mean look at me; you got the upper hand, man. Why would I lie to you?"

Rasim placed his hand on Navy's forehead as if he were checking his temperature. "Don't worry, man. I'm not going to kill you," he smiled.

Navy was surprised and delighted. "You not?"

"No," he said calmly.

He remained relieved until he recalled Rasim's legend in his mind. If Rasim was going to mark him, Navy wanted to suggest that he'd go on ahead and kill him instead. Mainly because when people saw his face he wouldn't last a day on the DC streets. His fears were realized when Rasim reached in the back pocket of his jeans and removed a switchblade.

"No," Navy screamed as he moved his head quickly from left to right in an attempt to stunt Rasim's groove. "Please don't! I'm begging you!"

"Hold him," Rasim said looking upon his men.

Chance gripped the top of his head while Brooklyn steadied the chin as Rasim cut into the left and right corner of his lips just enough. When he was done, Rasim punched Navy several times in the gut until he screamed out in pain, causing the muscles in his face to contract and the slits Rasim created to widen.

When Rasim was done, blood poured out of his face and spilled onto the silver table beneath him. These days Rasim was doing a better job of giving his award winning Glasgow smile. That was for sure. He had to give himself credit.

In no way was Navy the first. Many men roamed the streets of DC with a smile like Navy's. Some would say they were brothers.

Most of the time Rasim would allow a patient to wander, knowing that the victim wouldn't last a day without some young killer preying upon him and snuffing out his life in the hopes of gaining Rasim's favor. And Navy wouldn't be any different.

Brooklyn and Chance cut the ropes binding Navy's arms and legs and Navy slid off of the table and slammed against the floor on all fours, resembling the dog he was born to be.

"Get the fuck out," Rasim told him by way of a swift kick to the lower chin. "And enjoy what's left of your life."

Navy hustled up the stairs backwards, as if his greatest fear was niggas grabbing asses, instead of shooting bullets in his head.

When he was gone Rasim observed his men. He had been in charge for years and they respected and feared him greatly. It was mighty different from those lovely Strawberry Meadows days.

"We have to find Vance," Rasim reiterated.

"I'm already on it," Brooklyn nodded.

"You want us to put one in his brain when we do?" Chance asked.

"No. Bring him to me." Rasim turned to leave but Brooklyn stopped him.

"Look, before you dip, why didn't you stop when I honked my horn at you yesterday?"

"Yesterday?" he frowned. "I was up under Snow all night. You ain't see me."

"First off, when are you not up under Snow?" Chance kidded.

"Fuck you, nigga," Rasim joked with his brother.

"No seriously," Brooklyn interrupted. "I thought I saw you driving this white van down Minnesota Avenue. I was trying to get your attention but you ain't stop. Wasn't sure if a body was in the back or not and you needed my help."

"Wasn't me," Rasim repeated firmer.

"Sure looked like your Indian looking ass. The van pulled up at Martin's Supply Plant off of Benning Road. You should go see that nigga. Word to God, dude could be your stunt double."

Rasim brushed it off. Lately people had been claiming to see him and in places he simply wouldn't roam. He just figured a dude with similar features was a little too close for his comfort. For now shit was cool, just as long as the replica didn't try pulling rank using Rasim's stripes. "Like I said, it wasn't me. Now find Vance."

"I know you let 'ole boy go," Chance said. "Since you like dudes to sport the Glasgow smile like Jordans and shit." He paused. "But are you sure Navy won't go tell him we coming?"

"I'm praying he does. That's the only reason I let him go. Before coming down, I told Fish to stay on him when I let him up and don't let nobody kill him. So for real, it's just a matter of time."

Rasim was back in his truck and on BWI Parkway and then the dumbest shit happened. As he rolled past a construction site, his right wheel caught a nail.

"Fuck," he yelled slamming his hand against the steering wheel. He couldn't be without his truck so he decided to pull off the parkway onto the shoulder and look up the nearest garage with his navigation system.

He was in luck. A place called King Amongst Kings Body Shop was located off the next exit. Although he never patronized the spot, he decided to give it a chance. He figured it was luck because its name was an old saying he used frequently as a kid.

When he pulled up, a white man dressed in a butler uniform rushed outside with a glass of champagne on a silver tray. Dude grabbed the glass and the moment Rasim stepped out, he offered him the flute.

But Rasim gave up alcohol and weed long ago so that he could keep his wits about him in the streets. Still, he was impressed that some boss thought enough to offer such a classy service in the nation's capital. "I'm good," Rasim responded. "But thanks, man."

"Not a problem, sir," he replied placing the glass back on the tray before opening the door for him. "Right this way."

When Rasim stepped inside, he was pleasantly surprised. Everything outside seemed regular but it was all an illusion. The moment he walked in, he was transported from Washington, DC to what resembled a small palace in London. It was elegantly dressed with burgundy furniture and outlined in gold with huge King Chairs in every corner.

Impressive. Rasim nodded.

When he peeped the counter, he checked out the white marble along with the dark-skinned gorgeous cashier behind the register with a Colgate smile. Rasim stepped to her and she said, "Your wish is my command, sir? How may I serve you?"

If only she could bounce on his dick. Shit, that would be a good start.

Instead of giving her his inner needs, he shook his head, smiled and said, "How long this spot been open?" He glanced around again.

"A little over a month," she admitted. "But we have over fifty shops in and around the United States of America."

He nodded in approval. "Whoever the owner is, tell him I'm impressed."

"And what makes you think the owner is male?" a female asked as she made her way to the counter. At first she was about to kid the customer a bit more until she saw who he was. Right there, in the flesh, was the one man on the planet who stole and broke her heart in the same year.

Her acknowledgment of him came at the exact same time he remembered her. "Queen?" He leaned in. "Is that you?"

The last time he saw Queen was at Strawberry Meadows many moons ago. They had a little rendezvous in the laundry room but he left her high and dry as he hooked up with Snow instead.

Queen resented him for standing her up and her friends talked about it so much she had to cut their hating asses out of her life.

Queen never realized how much she cared about Rasim until he asked her to suck his dick in music class, and she did, only for him to run up in a tiny church looking for Flat Butt Snow Bradshaw.

Queen swaggered around the counter and stole a closer look at Rasim. All she could say was Good Gawd. He was only a reflection of the boy he used to be because what stood before her was spectacular. The muscles. The tattoos and even the Kufi and the scar over his eye gave him an appeal between hardened ex-convict and a hood fashion model.

The years hadn't been too bad on Queen either. Her face was unblemished and her long light brown hair trickled down her shoulders, stopping right at the entrance of her cleavage. Her tiny waist sat on top of her curvaceous hips and even from the front he could see that ass.

Rasim, who over the last decade was never physical with anyone but Snow, gripped her up and hugged her tightly in his arms. Her face nestled against his chest and she inhaled his cologne as if she owned the nigga. It wasn't long before her pussy moistened and she was begging with her eyes for him to fuck her on site.

Queen hadn't felt that much fire since the barbeque pit flipped over last summer at her crib and a piece of coal flew out and burnt the tip of her nose.

"I'm sorry," Rasim uttered realizing he had done way too much as it pertained to physical touch. "It's just good to see you that's all." He looked her over and could feel his dick stiffening. "So tell me what's going on? You married?"

"Yes," she admitted. "My husband owns a few banks in and around DC."

Rasim was disappointed and yet he didn't know why.

"What about you?" she asked.

When he remembered his wife, before he even sniffed Queen's pussy, he felt like he was cheating. The smile disappeared off of his face as he recalled the look in her eyes the last time he broke her heart at Hains Point. "Yeah," he nodded. "I married Snow and shit."

Although Queen was grinning, she was whispering *I hate that bitch* inside. She had been in love with Rasim so long that she named her business after hearing his favorite saying in the laundry room the day he lost his virginity to Snow. But she never thought she would see him again.

It was because of Snow's dry, flat-butt, no-personality-having ass that she never got to experience Rasim beyond sucking his dick in class. Maybe it was time for a little revenge.

"Well, I'm happy to hear that," she lied before focusing on her employee. "Lisa, give Mr. Nami one of my business cards." The cashier did as instructed. "If you ever need assistance, for anything," Queen looked into his eyes, "call me." The cashier slipped it in his hand.

Rasim tucked the card in his back pocket and he would remember the intensity she used to make the comment when he was punishing Snow later that night.

"Now let me get you some service," Queen said slyly as she licked her upper lip. "For your truck, that is."

CHAPTER 14

SNOW

Snow and Mute Candy were chilling in a booth at The Cheesecake Factory in Towson, Maryland while Amber and Cassie went shopping for their graduation outfits within the connecting mall.

Mute Candy had not only given Donald's daughters all of the love she could spare, but she added her attention to detail to make sure his twins prospered in home and in life. Nobody had better lay a hand on them like the pervert did when he tried to rape her many seasons ago. It would be un-good and she knew that wasn't a word.

Mute Candy was so dedicated to their lives that both received full scholarships to Spelman College in Atlanta and that included room and board.

Amber, the dainty one out of the two, was taking Biology with a minor in Japanese Studies while Cassie elected to major in Computer Software and Information Sciences.

With the money the girls received from the September 11th Victims Compensation Fund, coupled with the dough Rasim, Chance and Brooklyn dropped on them as if it were going out of style, they wouldn't have to want for a thing. And as heavy as their bank accounts were at the moment, that may be the case for the rest of their lives.

The fellas weren't just popping shit when they vowed to be in the twins' lives on the day Donald took his last breath. They saw them at least three times a week and attended school meetings. That also included Basketball games when Cassie displayed her vicious dunking abilities and the talent shows where Amber showcased her singing chops. Whenever they glanced in any audience, in any part of the world, Rasim, Brooklyn and Chance were always in front row seats.

At one point, Mute Candy had to go on the fellas, especially Rasim, for buying gifts for the girls without warrant. She wanted them to work for their spoils instead of expecting everything to be handed to them. But every now and again, because the girls were so smart, and so respectful, she'd allow them access to the expensive gifts, which was why both of them sported Louis Vuitton purses on their arms today.

They even blessed her with money and when she wouldn't take it they would deposit it in her bank account.

"If I keep the baby he will leave me," Snow said as she sat across from Mute Candy and spoke in sign language about her latest pinch. She was pregnant yet again. "He specifically said he doesn't want a child in the world, only so some nigga with a vendetta could use him or her against him. And I feel him."

"He should have pulled out then," she signed.

"Mute Candy!"

"I'm serious." Mute Candy rolled her eyes and moaned a little like she did whenever she got upset. "Your baby is a gift, Snow. It's not a pair of shoes you can take back to the mall when they don't fit," she signed hard. "You're worried about what Ras feels when your logic is off. If anything, you should be concerned about God and the way you keep breaking His heart by eliminating His precious gifts from your body." She paused. "You can't get another abortion, my friend. Not this time."

Snow never told Rasim about the first abortion to protect his heart and she never would.

Still, Snow thought about what Mute Candy signed and she knew it would be unethical but her relationship was going so well with her husband that this kind of thing could set them back five years. Especially when he expressed how he felt about the matter in the past.

Snow loved the Lord. That was true. But what they didn't know was that she worshiped Rasim with the same vigor. With the same passion and that was dangerous.

She was about to leave and think about the matter at home when Rasim bopped into the restaurant with a bitch. Confused on why he was there, Snow frowned and looked down at her gold Rolex watch. It was two o'clock in the afternoon and he told her earlier that day that he was going out of town.

Slowly she stood up from her seat to address the affair properly. Mute Candy was signing and trying to figure out what was up with the baby until Snow was on her feet.

Did dude have the audacity to cheat again? Snow thought.

Out of nervousness, she kept swallowing until she was upon his back. With her heart swirling in her stomach, she tapped him on the shoulder and whispered, "Rasim."

When he turned around, in her error, she was forced to take two steps backwards. The boy/man before her was not Rasim. Although similar in structure, he was much smaller now that she was upon him. In addition, he was younger.

"Can I help you?" he asked in a kind voice.

BY T. STYLES

Snow perused his features carefully. They were not original. Rasim Nami was the real owner. Because the young man before her looked just like Rasim when she first met him in Strawberry Meadows. She was experiencing Deja Vu. How was that possible?

"No…uh…I thought you were someone else."

He smiled and said, "Since I've been home from college, I've been hearing that a lot."

Snow tried to grin back but her cheeks felt heavy. Was this boy Rasim's son? And if so did he know?

Rasim and Snow sat quietly at the table across from one another in their home. He desired seafood gumbo and since his wish was her command, she made him a big delicious pot.

Snow decided to keep the boy/man secret because she had other things to talk to him about.

Although he was tearing through his food as if he hadn't eaten a bite all day, she was chasing a shrimp in her bowl. Her appetite vanished just like the years they spent together in their marriage.

Not feeling Snow's altered state, Rasim devoured the last piece of garlic bread, wiped his mouth with the napkin and said, "What's on your mind, Snow?"

"I'm pregnant," she blurted out.

Damn!

When she rehearsed in the mirror she had a different script. Unfortunately she forgot her lines and, as a result, fumbled.

"You pregnant?" he frowned sitting up straight in his chair. "Fuck you mean you pregnant? I thought we discussed that we weren't having any kids. Ever!"

"We did, Rasim, but—"

"But what?" he yelled as if she were an out casted nigga on the block. "You decided that you weren't going to listen to me? That you weren't going to follow my command? Fuck wrong with you Snow?"

The way he was carrying on, you'd think she fucked herself.

"That's not fair, Rasim," she said as tears built themselves up in the wells of her eyes. "It takes two to get pregnant so this is not all my fault."

Rasim slammed his fist on the table, causing both bowls to topple to the floor. He stood up and his increased height intimidated her. "If you want to stay married to me, you will get an abortion tomorrow. If not, then I'll go down and file for divorce." He pointed at the door. "I will never bring a child in this world, only to suffer a loss like I did when my parents died. Make a decision, Snow, because on that, I will not waiver!" He stormed away and slammed their bedroom door.

CHAPTER 15

RASIM

Rasim slouched in the parking lot of Martin's Supply Plant in his truck feeling as if the fate of the world was on his shoulders. He had a lot of shit on his mind and he knew he didn't need to add more but yet he needed to know. Was the man resembling him roaming around Washington, DC his son?

As he readjusted himself in his seat, he thought about Snow and how he talked to her a few days ago. He hated to force her to get an abortion the other day, but he was a drug lord with enemies and he couldn't stand the idea of someone kidnapping his child to get at him. He didn't even go with her for the procedure.

To make shit worse, he was scouring the city for another child. He wasn't even certain what his plan was if the boy/man he was stalking was his seed.

Unfortunately for Rasim, he didn't have the benefit of a Deadbeat Dad gene in his body. His father was honorable. His father took care of his child and although the boy/man was an adult, wouldn't he be required to do the same?

Something else was bothering Rasim that he was feeling mad guilty about. Since he last saw Queen, he had been wondering about her ever since. Well, pondering her pussy really.

The boredom of his existing relationship was weighing on him and he needed some excitement. Just one hint of adventure! But would it cost him everything? He couldn't see the price tag so for now he could only answer yes.

When the lights went off in the supply store and someone came out, Rasim scooted down in his seat. As he peered through the windshield, he saw someone as tall as him strut out. But when the boy/man turned his head, slightly to the right, he saw his own face.

He didn't need a DNA test. He was blood.

Rasim threw the car door open and dipped out just as Selena was pulling up to pick him up. But when she saw Rasim approaching her son, she thought she was losing her mind. She parked any kind of way, hopped out and stepped in front of Rasim with pleading eyes. "Rasim, please don't."

"Is he who I think he is?" Rasim asked, huffing and puffing.

"Mom, what's going on?" her son asked standing behind her while the man who was his father stared him down for points.

She turned around and said, "Stanley, go get in the car."

"But, mom—"

"Stanley, go get in the fucking car!" she yelled.

Defeated, he stole one more look at Rasim and then obeyed his mother's request.

Although Selena stood before him wearing a pink dress with her titties spilling out, an outfit that would've set him back to fucking her in the past, Rasim's attention remained over her head, and on his seed, as he hustled to the car.

BY T. STYLES

When Stanley was inside, Rasim, still eyeing him inside the car, asked, "Is he mine, Selena?"

"Yes," she said lowering her head. "But can we go somewhere and talk? And I'll tell you everything you want to know." Rasim didn't budge, as he felt responsible for the years he missed even though it wasn't his fault. "Please, Rasim."

Somehow, in some way, Selena convinced Rasim to go back to his truck and talk to her. She wanted to go to a restaurant but he would never be seen with her alone, only for Snow to find out and leave him again. Especially since she wasn't married anymore.

Drooped behind the steering wheel, Rasim continued to eye the car that held his son. His good eye twitched because he was so enraged. What kind of hateful, stupid, dumb bitch could keep a man from his own child?

A father was required to school his son in the ways of the world. A father needed to be there for his boy and mold his thinking patterns when he was young, to give him the basics on code and honor. Any later and it might be too late. Was she that reckless and selfish that she couldn't understand mere Father-Son Philosophy?

"Why did you lie? Huh?" He glared at her. "Why did you have me thinking I didn't have a son when I did? I specifically asked you, Selena, and you said no! Why?" His voice was high pitched. "Was I that terrible that you thought I wouldn't want to be in his life?"

Of course had he known, he would've suggested an abortion but hindsight was twenty-twenty.

She sighed. "I didn't want to ruin my relationship," she whispered. "I was married at the time and Rodney would've flipped if he thought Stanley wasn't his."

"But he don't look shit like that nigga," Rasim yelled.

He saw her husband at a strip club a few years back and he could only wish he could be responsible for a boy/man as handsome as Stanley. He looked like two types of Notorious BIG.

The shit was dumb!

"The boy has my face, Selena! What the fuck!" He slammed his fist into his steering wheel causing it to honk.

"I know, Rasim, I know. And I'm so sorry. I got pregnant when you were at Strawberry Meadows and I met him the next day after you and I had sex. We had been to-gether ever since and things moved so quickly—"

"And you fucking lied to me to be a fucking wife," he said cutting her off.

Rasim's nostrils flared and his breathing pattern grew noisy. He hated the feelings he was experiencing. No, he didn't want children. And yes, openly having a child with Selena could have destroyed his chances of remaining Snow's husband. But Stanley was his son and the man in him would not allow anybody to come in the way of that, not even Snow.

He laughed out of disgust for the stupid bitch and shook his head. "How is he? I mean…what kind of man is he?"

Selena sighed. "He rolls with the wrong people sometimes but…I mean…other than that, he's trying."

Rasim nodded his head. He always imagined if he had a child it would look like him but he didn't know the resemblance would be uncanny.

"Rasim, I truly apologize," she said eyeing him. The moonlight coming through the window gave her a good view and she couldn't believe how sexy he had gotten over the years. If he looked like one ounce of this in the past, Snow would have been in trouble.

And then she had an idea. In the pits of her mind, she knew Snow wasn't fucking him like she could so it was time for her to remind him.

"I can't believe how handsome you got. Now you built like Superman."

Rasim shook his head. "In Snow's mind, I was always Superman. That's why she's my wife."

She placed her hand on his bulging bicep. Fuck Snow. She was going for hers. "You got me remembering the old times." She licked her lips and rubbed his arm. "What do you say we—"

He gripped her fingers and squeezed them so hard she winced. "Bitch, don't ever in your fucked up life touch me again. Do you hear me? I'm a married man and even if I wasn't I wouldn't fuck with you." He hit the power unlock button. "Now get the fuck out of my truck before I cock and tug on your slutty ass," he said tapping the handle of the gun nestled in his waist. "I'll be in contact later about my son."

Embarrassed, Selena rolled her eyes, opened the door, got out and slammed it shut. Before walking away, she threw both fuck you fingers in the air for good measure and stomped to her ride.

Selena could perform all she wanted. The only thing on Rasim's mind was what he was going to tell Snow, especially since she had an abortion due to his stance on having children.

Well, since he was already in trouble, he didn't see the problem with going a little deeper and getting some pussy too. What could be the harm in that?

The craziest thing happened. After leaving Selena, Rasim's tire was gashed and as a result he had to visit Queen to get it fixed. Of course he tore the bitch open himself. And yes, he stopped by 7-Eleven before meeting her to purchase a pack of condoms. But if someone asked, he would swear before God and all the moons that it was not true.

The meeting started out honestly enough. Rasim called Queen, told her about his ordeal and she met him at her shop. But not even five minutes later, her hands were on the table while his paws were on her waist as he fucked her viciously from behind.

After all the years, after all the heartache, she was finally being blessed with Rasim Nami's dick. Queen rotated her hips and pushed back into Rasim like she was dancing.

Oh the joy!

Oh the feeling!

When it started getting too good, she pressed her right foot on top of the desk while the other stayed planted on the floor. This caused her pussy to tighten on the right thereby squeezing Rasim's dick in the process.

Queen's fuck game was top notch. None of that lazy shit some chicks did nowadays.

Rasim was older but still time enough for her. He stirred the insides of her box like the big spoon to white cake batter. The warmer she got, the tighter she got, and the more shit she talked, the more she made him forget that he was a married man.

At the moment he was taken back to the olden days. It was as if she was a bitch, and he was a hood nigga, and they made an executive decision to straight fuck.

"I'm 'bout to cum," he announced and squeezed her hips so hard he would leave fingerprints later. "Shit!"

As if Rasim's dick was on fire, she pushed him backwards forcing him to frown for killing the moment. Suddenly his pulsating dick was out in the open, like the ugly girl at a party, until she dropped to her knees, ripped the condom off and allowed him to rest in peace in her throat.

Her warm tongue circled the shaft and she sucked as if trying to gain milkshake from a straw.

In ecstasy, Rasim placed his hands on the sides of her head and pumped into her until every drop of semen was in the pit of her gut.

That shit was perfect!

In his original itinerary, he thought he would feel bad about fucking Queen, go back to his wife, and humble himself before Snow. But when Queen stood up and smiled, he figured what was the harm in staying a little while? Besides, Queen wasn't some stranger or layabout on the street. She was familiar. She represented his past and she didn't mind reminding him that although she relished in the man who stood before her today, she was still attracted to him when he was younger.

So instead of going home, instead of taking the memories and moving on with his life, he stayed.

After they fucked, he ordered a pizza and they ate the entire thing in her office. He hadn't remembered her being so engaging; then again, he didn't give her a chance.

Rasim sat back in the seat and held a slice in his right hand while his left rested against his dick. Every so often a good memory would return about the session they just experienced and Rasim would look over at Queen and tremble.

He knew he was supposed to leave and that holding a conversation was breaking code but she was married, and judging by the rock on her finger, he surmised that her husband adored her very much.

Alas, he found the one person in Washington, DC with just as much to lose.

Queen sat on the floor of her office and leaned against the wall. Her legs spread slightly so that he could see the sleekness of her drippy pussy. Her expensive weave sat in a messy ponytail on top of her head and for whatever reason Rasim was grinning from ear to ear.

"What you thinking about over there, boy?"

He chuckled and finished what was left of his slice. "Boy?" He paused as he brushed his hands together to get rid of the crumbs. "Naw, sexy. I'm all man."

"You think I'm sexy now?" she grinned licking her lips.

"You already know the answer to that. Plus you always been sexy to me."

She smiled but not too brightly. "So you know after giving me some of that good dick that I'm gonna want it again, right? I hope you not gonna hold back, Rasim. Let's be there for each other in this crazy world."

"As long as you act right, we good."

"Act right?" She paused before nibbling her pizza. "What about my fuck game would cause you to think I'd act any other way?"

"Nothing." He sat up and rested his elbows on his knees. Then he clasped his fingers together. "I just don't want this to get too heavy. I never cheated on my wife since we been married. This shit right here is a first." He pointed at the floor.

"So that makes me special?" she responded.

"It makes you worthy." He looked down at his boots and then back at her again. "But I need you to be who you are always and never change. Don't fuck with my marriage. Don't fuck with my wife. And let shit play out. Can you handle that?"

"Time will show you better than I can say." She tossed the pizza on the floor and crawled over to him. "But first let me lick that dick clean. I don't want any remnants of me on your stick when you go home."

Queen sucked his dick so well that he was forced into a stupor and stole a nap. While his eyes rested, something he would've never done in the past, she snapped a few pictures for her collection.

Little did Rasim know, Queen was married back in the day. But the husband she owned left years ago due to her floozy ways.

Prior to running in to Rasim she had a FOR SALE sign on her pussy. But now that she had him, even if he didn't know it, she considered herself SOLD.

CHAPTER 16

SNOW

Snow ensconced herself on the sofa as she clutched her fingers together.

She didn't feel well.

Something vicious pushed itself into her home, into her life, and into her marriage. It was ingesting her from the inside out. She wasn't sure but she had a feeling it involved Rasim and someone else.

In the beginning she thought her sorrow stemmed from having to abort yet another of Rasim's bairns. The first of which, he never found out about. But now, well now she knew it was something much darker and it took the shape of a woman.

When Rasim stepped into the house he was holding his dick because he had to piss badly. He kissed Snow on the cheek and said, "Let me drain the weasel right quick, baby. I'll be right back." He ran inside and closed the door.

Snow trudged to the bathroom and placed her earlobe against the panel. There was a firm reason. She was listening for the pause that occurred in a man's piss stream after he just busted a nut. If his urine canal was clear and he hadn't cum within that hour, his elimination would be steady without interruption. But if he had fucked recently his urine would hesitate and come out in big drops due to being clogged.

BY T. STYLES

And at the moment Rasim's piss was coming out like a leaky faucet.

Dirty ass nigga. She thought.

When he exited the bathroom she was standing in the middle of the floor. She fiddled with her fingernails and her shoulders were as stiff as a poker stick. "Rasim," she said delicately, "who is she?"

Rasim maintained face but his stomach swirled and twirled to the point where he had to go to the bathroom again. This time to shit. He couldn't make a quick retreat just yet though. He had to be smart. Besides, why did Snow suspect anything? He came home every night for dinner on time. He never stayed out later than normal and he instructed Queen to fall back on makeup and perfume if she wanted to see him.

"Baby, I don't know what you talking 'bout." He treaded toward her but not close enough to lay hands.

Her brows lowered and her lips tightened. "You stink of funky whore," she said, her voice tougher than the hardest nigga.

Worried she caught him red-handed, Rasim moved closer and said, "Snow, you know I wouldn't—"

"Beware, my dear husband," she said cutting him off. "If I find her this time I will smoke her out," she said pointing a strong finger in his face. "So do yourself a favor while you still can." She paused. "And rid yourself of the funky bitch!"

CHAPTER 17

RASIM

R asim sat at a table in an apartment where he conducted his dope business. They found Vance's whereabouts and now they had to get their hands on him. Just as he thought, Navy went to visit Vance a few days after Rasim's patchwork, which gave him the face of the Joker.

Brooklyn and Chance were going to snatch him but Vance had two FBI agents protecting him at all times. So Rasim would have to find another way but it had to be soon.

Although serious business was on the table, the only thing on his mind at the moment was Snow. He knew she didn't have any solid facts that he was cheating but her woman's intuition caused him to ignore Queen longer than he planned.

It had been a week since Queen saw Rasim. At first she called every other day but after the first week she left him alone. She figured if he wanted to cut her out of his life then she would back off and try another approach, at another time.

Her silence was working because Rasim missed her sweet pussy and the way she clenched his dick when she activated her Kegel muscle exercises during sex. It wasn't that he was falling in love with her. It was just that Queen provided the spice he needed to secure the longevity of his marriage.

Whether Snow knew it or not, Queen's very presence was saving their relationship. But he knew Snow didn't want to hear that shit.

Rasim was leaning back in his chair looking at Brooklyn and Chance when his cell phone rang on the table. He picked it up, looked at the number and saw it was his wife. Reluctantly he answered. "I'll be home in a minute."

"Rasim, come home now," she demanded.

He could tell by her voice that something was up so he instructed his men to keep a lookout on Vance's house and that when the opportunity provided itself that they should snatch him out by his eyelids.

Afterwards, he jumped in his truck and his phone rang again. This time it was Queen and he was surprised at how pleased he was to see her number. He raised the handset next to his head and said, "What up?"

"Hey, Rasim," she said in a sweet voice. "I'm not calling to bother you. Just wanted to make sure you were okay."

He smiled a little. "I'm fine, sexy. Thanks for asking."

"Alright. Talk to you later."

Click.

What the fuck? Was this chick serious? She hung up without another word and he missed her already. If she was playing a game she was good at it because he appreciated her restraint.

So he called back. "What you doing tomorrow?" he asked.

"You if you want me," she said softly.

"I'll meet you at your shop."

"I'll see you then."

When he hung up, suddenly he had something to look forward to. Now all he had to do was see what got his wife so riled up that she would pull him from work.

Rasim parked his truck, slipped out and approached his house. But when he saw Selena in the living room, sitting on his couch at that, he started to put his hands around her neck like a tight scarf.

He tossed is keys on the table next to the door and rushed toward her like she broke into his house. That was until Snow yelled, "Rasim, sit down." When he didn't stop, she said, "Please!"

When Rasim focused on his wife's eyes he could tell she was more concerned than angry. Maybe Selena wasn't there claiming they fucked.

With his eyes stuck on Selena like duct tape to a kidnap victim's lips, he waited for her to say a wrong word, just one, so he could tuck her face under his boot. "What you doing in my house, Selena?" he asked through heavy breaths and clenched teeth.

"I'm here about your son."

Rasim observed Snow's expression and her mood hadn't changed. He expected more from her especially since he never told her he had a child. Or in this instance, a man.

"I saw him one day, Rasim. When you weren't around." She exhaled. "I knew all along."

Wow. That shocked Rasim.

"What about my son, Selena?" he asked returning his attention to the whore.

"He was arrested," she said wiping the sweat off of her brow.

"For what?"

"Robbing a church."

He stood up. "Robbing a church? What the fuck you talking 'bout?"

She exhaled. "All of Stanley's life I tried to keep him away from the bad elements of DC. I put him in private schools and when it was time for college I made sure it was out of town. But whenever he came home, he always got up with the same friends."

"What was his part in all this shit?" he asked through clenched lips.

"He was the getaway driver. And when he was locked up and offered a deal, his time was lessened."

"Offered a deal?" Rasim repeated as the muscles in his jaw twitched. "Are you saying he snitched?"

"I don't choose those words but if you do, then yes," she responded. "And I'm here because once his friends find out they will kill him in prison." She paused. "I mean can you talk to some of your friends to protect him? He's in Cumberwoods."

Rasim did a brief stint in that penitentiary so he was hip on the ways of the land. In fact, when he was allowed probation on an assault charge he was given recently, he was instructed that if he ever came back he would have to finish out the year left on his sentence.

Rasim rubbed his scalp and said, "I need to think things through with my wife. I'll be in contact with you later."

"But, Rasim, I need your—"

"Get the fuck up out my house," he roared. "You already overstepped your boundaries by coming here."

Selena knew his parents' address, which was how she found him.

PRISON THRONE

Grief-stricken, Selena stood up with tears in her eyes. "I know you're upset with me for not telling you. But right or wrong, he is still your son and I need your help. We need your help. I hope I can count on you."

Selena was beside herself with tears when Snow walked slowly over to her. Once she was in her face, instead of embracing her in a hug, Snow slapped her in the face and punched her in the gut.

Selena dropped to the floor and held her belly.

"The slap was for the shit you pulled down Hains Point," Snow said looking upon her with zero pity. "And the punch was for having a child by my husband and not telling him." She opened the door. "Now get up out my house."

When she crawled out, Snow helped her with a foot shove, slammed the door and leaned against it. Rasim walked over to his wife and caressed the tops of her shoulders. "Snow, I'm so sorry."

"When did you find out?" she asked looking up at him.

"Some weeks back. People kept telling me that I had someone who looked like me and I never went to check before recently. But when I saw his eyes, I knew it was him. I don't even need a blood test, baby. I'm so sorry. It happened during Strawberry Meadows when you first left me."

Snow lowered her head. "Everybody got a child by you but me."

Rasim lifted her chin slightly with the push of his finger. "Not everybody, just one. But you gotta believe I'm not fucking that bitch, Snow. I can't even stand her."

She exhaled and raised her head to look into his eyes. "You know what, before she came over I thought you were. But when I saw how you looked at her, when you came in the house, I knew it was impossible. The last time I saw that expression on your face was the day you killed Levi." She wrapped her hands around his muscular body. "I'm sorry I didn't believe you, Rasim. You've been such a good husband and I'm blind with jealousy." She tucked her face into his chest. "Can you ever forgive me?"

Rasim was torn. Part of him felt guilty but the other part that was closer to his dick was relieved that she would no longer think he was cheating.

"Snow, don't worry about it," he said as he embraced her and massaged her back. "We'll be alright."

She gripped him tighter and spoke into his chest. "So what are we going to do? About your son?"

"I don't know. But I'm hoping something comes to me soon."

Rasim was lying on the bed naked, with his hand on his stomach. He was in a hotel room with Queen and her leg was draped across his legs while her head was nestled in his chest.

With Snow not suspecting him of cheating, he increased his game and rented a hotel for the day in Delaware. They had been fucking nonstop and he would've still been asleep if he hadn't experienced an unpleasant dream.

In his nightmare his father came to him while he was sitting on top of a hill. His message for his son was simple. That Rasim had to violate his probation and return to prison or Stanley would be murdered in a month's time.

Lately he had been seeing his father during his daily travels. He knew it was just a matter of time before he had a conversation with him so he wasn't surprised to see him in his dreams, just confused.

When he eased from up under Queen, who was sound asleep, he walked into the bathroom to piss. He had no idea that she had been faking the entire time.

On some sneak shit as she heard his urine splash into the toilet, she crept out of bed and tiptoed toward her purse. Queen removed a business card, folded it multiple times and slid it into the small inner pocket inside of his jeans.

She believed that even if Rasim dug inside of his pockets throughout the day that he would not go in the tiny concealed pocket. But she was sure Snow would eventually.

BY T. STYLES

CHAPTER 18

SNOW

Snow and Rasim sat in a dark restaurant inside of the Four Seasons Hotel. The all black suit he modeled set off the dark features of his smooth face, including his growing beard.

Snow was equally enchanting and the red dress she wore exposed just enough cleavage to cause neighboring male customers to look her way every so often to be sure she was still there. "Husband," she said placing her hand over his, which held his fork. "What's on your mind?"

He exhaled. "I want to talk to you about something but I don't know how you gonna react."

She removed her hand and wiped her mouth with the white cloth napkin even though nothing was on her lips. "Just tell me, Rasim." She cleared her throat, fearing the worst. "Let's start there."

"I'm worried about Stanley."

She leaned in. "Stanley?"

"My son."

She sat back and sighed.

Hearing the words *MY SON* egress from his mouth and knowing she had nothing to do with his birth panged her. "What is it about someone you haven't formally met that could keep you so tight, and so tense, that you would keep it from me?" She paused. "Over the past few weeks you've been growing the hair out on your face and you refuse to give me any attention. What the fuck is up?"

He sat back in the seat and puffed. "Snow, whether or not I met him doesn't negate the fact that he is my son. What do you want me to do? Turn my back on someone I helped bring into this world?"

"You mean someone you helped bring into this world because you were cheating?"

"I mean someone I helped bring into this world that has my blood in his veins regardless of my faithfulness to you," he yelled. "I was a kid, baby. I'm sorry."

She touched her stomach and tried to prevent the ugly cry from occurring. "Rasim, I don't think I can handle this."

"Handle what?" he frowned. "You haven't even given me a chance to tell you what's on my mind and you're already being difficult."

She slammed her napkin down. "I'm listening! Tell me what's so important that you would continue to cause me pain."

He shook his head and wiped his hand down his beard. He was trying to be sensitive to his wife's feelings but the melodrama level was high. After all, it wasn't easy knowing that he produced something with the one human on planet earth she hated most of all.

"I might have to turn myself in to prison to protect him. That's why I've been growing out the hair on my face. If I go inside I want to look as differently from him as possible." He paused. "I know this is tough but Selena not telling me about my kid was not his fault, Snow. He'll die without my help. I have to do this."

He poured his heart out and the only thing Snow heard was that her husband was leaving her. "Turn yourself in? How, Rasim?"

"By violating my probation."

"If you do that you'll be inside for at least a year," she yelled hoping to bring him back to his senses. "What about me? What about us?"

"I know but I don't have any choice."

She sat back and looked over at him. "Rasim, you can't violate your probation." She leaned over the table. "Especially with everything you're facing." She knocked three times on the table to signal their code word for the FBI. She was trying to remind him of Vance, who was still on the lamb. What if he was locked up and they kept him there? "And what if someone tries to kill you."

"Never," he said arrogantly. Rasim was a legend and in prison he sat on the throne.

"But it could happen. Even the impossible does."

"I don't have a choice, Snow. The only reason I can't do it right now is because I can't get to Vance." He paused. "But once I do, I'm gone."

"Sounds like the decision is already made to me."

Silence.

"I had no business marrying you," she said in a low voice.

"I'm sorry you feel that way." He touched her hand and she jerked it away. Besides, she needed it to wipe her upcoming tears.

"Snow, I know this is fucked up. I know you're hurting but do you want the kind of man who could deny his own child?"

She didn't respond.

"Do you?"

PRISON THRONE

"No," she said through clenched teeth. "I want the kind of man who would have never had a child on me in the first place." She wiped her mouth again, threw the napkin in his face and stormed out.

Snow declared war.

She didn't speak to him and he didn't speak to her despite conducting business together.

Snow was hoping that her silence would force him to realize how stupid he was being. But he moved about the home like she wasn't even a factor. And in the second week he did something that in all of the years they were married he never did before.

He failed to come home.

When Snow rolled over and her husband was not in the bed, she felt like she'd been gut punched. He won. He succeeded in proving her point and Snow knew it was time to wave the flag. Because although she was as tough as rawhide, when it came to a real man and his child she wasn't prepared to wager her marriage. So she called him and said, "Okay, Rasim. I concede. Please come home."

"I'm on my way."

Rasim got there an hour later. He stood in the middle of the floor and stared down at his beautiful but depressed wife. What she didn't know was that although he missed her terribly, he could've stretched the beef out a month longer if she wanted the trouble. Besides, he had worthy company. Although Queen was no replacement, she was a good sideline.

BY T. STYLES

"Thank you, Snow." He gripped her into a warm embrace. "Thank you so much." He rocked her in his arms in the middle of the living room floor.

He felt differently to Snow in her mind but she couldn't figure out why.

When he released her he said, "Now all I gotta do is get this nigga Vance and I'll be straight." He rubbed his beard. "With this nigga out there, I can't even leave right now if I wanted to."

Snow sighed and shook her head.

"What's wrong?" he asked.

She dug in her pocket, opened his palm and slapped a key in his hand. Afterwards she dipped into her other pocket and handed him an address off of Martin Luther King Jr. Blvd. "You'll find him there. In the basement. Tied up and waiting for you."

He thought she was fucking around because she spoke as if she were giving him driving instructions. "Snow, are you telling me the nigga I've been searching for forever is at this address?"

She nodded. "He's been there a week."

Whoa. She kept him hidden knowing Rasim wouldn't go back to prison without him.

Instead of getting mad, he was relieved. "Baby, do you fucking realize what you've done?" he asked excitedly. "You saved my life."

"I'm your wife, Rasim." She looked into his eyes so that he could feel the weight of what that really meant. "It's my duty to protect you. Like it's your duty to protect me. Isn't that what we vowed?" She touched the place where her name rested on his chest.

Her remark hit him in the heart because at the moment he was being a world-class whore. "Yes it's my duty to protect you, Snow. And no matter what goes on, I always will."

"I hope you mean it, Rasim."

He ran his finger down the side of her face. "Of course I do." He paused. "But, baby, how did you get him?" he questioned trying to skip the subject.

"It was easy." She shrugged. "Some men have a penchant for new pussy." She glared at him. "And in Vance's case, he'll pay for it with his life."

CHAPTER 19

RASIM

In three days Rasim would violate his probation to return to prison and save his son's life. And although he was having second thoughts, the choice did not belong to him anymore. It was a must. If Rasim didn't help him, his son would perish.

He was standing in the middle of a hotel room at the W holding Queen in his arms because she was crying like the slut baby she was. This would be the last time he'd see her for a year and she was butt naked and beside herself with grief.

He had broken so many codes when it came to Queen that it was impossible to find the proper place to start. For one, he allowed himself to spend too much time without getting the necessary intel on her background. Was she really married? Was she happy? And did she have ulterior motives?

The tragedy was that Rasim was astute. He knew things didn't add up but he still kept her around. He realized that Queen didn't move in the world like a woman who had a husband. Whenever he wanted to see her, no matter the hour, she was available. He even brought up her flexibility one day and asked how her husband felt.

"He's fine," she would say dismissing the matter. "He trusts me."

Rasim believed what he wanted. Besides, it was cool having two women.

But just picturing Snow leaving their home anytime she wanted without him being with her was hard to fathom. He demanded too much of her time and relied on her for his existence. Snow had to prepare dinner every night. Snow washed his clothes and dropped to her knees to fulfill every sexual desire. That didn't include the things she did for the drug operation. She was in charge of making sure the mules who ran dope up and down the coast were paid. And she was in charge of getting them attorneys if they were arrested so they wouldn't cave. She was good at it too so there was never any free time.

What did her husband require?

Rasim wondered, although Queen wore a beautiful ring, did her husband really fuck with her at all?

"I'm going to miss you so much," she said looking up at him, her face wet with tears. "My pussy too," she cooed. "And I know you aren't mine, and I know this isn't right but I'll still be worried when you go inside."

"Come on, Queen," he said wiping the water off of her face with the back of his hand. "I know you dealt with a dude in prison before. You know a year is a cakewalk. Why you so uptight?"

"No I haven't," she admitted. "This is the first time this has ever happened to me, Rasim. My husband is a white collar type dude so it ain't the same."

"Well don't worry, sexy. I'll be in contact every day. We won't miss a beat." He ran his cool hand down her back. "Trust me."

"You saying that but I don't believe you," she pouted. "You probably got a rack of bitches who'll be taking up your time. I need to feel special, Rasim. That's how this shit works between you and me. I just hope you're not collecting hearts like you did mine."

That's the only thing that frustrated him about Queen. For some reason in the back of her mind she assumed he bedded a lot of women. It probably had more to do with the fact that he was cheating period. Lately he spent more time than he wanted explaining that although he loved being inside of her, he wasn't a whore off the street. He was a man with money and too much to lose to fuck with chicken heads. It just wasn't his thing.

He reminded her repeatedly that he chose her because he had a second place position available and he wanted to fill it with the right one. That's where she came in. She applied and was hired the day she sucked his nut down her throat.

Didn't she see that?

"Queen, I will be in contact." He rubbed her shoulders. He kissed her on the cheek and his beard tickled her lips. "That's my word."

She stroked his large bicep. "Why can't I see you right before you go in? Like the day of?"

Not this shit again, he thought as he exhaled.

All night Queen had been begging to see him the day before he went into prison and each time he said no. She could ask in any language around the world if she desired and the answer would always be the same.

Those last moments belong to Snow and he would never deny her. Not for a bitch in second place.

All Queen was trying to do was pull rank and see where she stood. And it was still behind his wife.

"I can't do that," he said walking away from her to slide on his watch. "This was our time together and I hope you enjoyed it as much as I did." When he was dressed he

PRISON THRONE

moved toward the door. "Goodbye, sexy. I'll see you in a year." He strutted out.

Queen remained planted in the middle of the floor with her drizzling pussy. "Naw, nigga." She hugged herself like a lunatic. "You gonna see me before that. I guarantee it."

She got on the phone and called a friend to help with her plan.

The stench of gunpowder twirled through the air in the warehouse as Rasim stood over Navy's body. Thanks to Snow, he was able to close some loose ends before returning to prison later that week. Since he already had Navy wearing his signature, it was time to put him out of his misery. Now he wore two bullets to the clavicle.

With Navy dead, he moved over to Vance who sat in a chair in the center of the floor. His arms were tied behind his back and a tire was draped around his neck. For an hour the tire was doused in gasoline and it was ready for his plan.

Rasim stared down at Vance with a hard smile resting on his face. To him, a man who snitched after obtaining money and success from the dope game that fed him was disposable. And the plan was to teach him a painful and final lesson.

Brooklyn and Chance stood behind the chief but both kept their eyes on the floor, each afraid to see the new limits Rasim would journey to today. Over the years Rasim's passion for maltreatment had reached astounding levels and they feared it would only get worse.

After 9/11, and losing his parents and Donald on the same day, Rasim didn't just grow stronger and richer, he also grew bitter. He blamed many Americans, the citizens and even Al-Qaeda for his suffering and he took his soreness out on people who owed him money.

"Rasim, I'm begging you, please don't do this," Vance begged as he inhaled the strong fumes. His goggle eyes peered up at Rasim who was so enraged he was steaming.

"Do what?" he responded cocking his head slightly to the side. "Punish you for getting in bed with the FBI? Or for stacking your pockets with cash, setting the empire on fire and then running out to save your own life? Which part are you asking mercy for?"

"I promise you, Rasim." His breaths were rapid and the gasoline was causing his eyes to burn. "All I was going to do was give them the information that wouldn't hurt you." He blinked a few times. "Light block shit, you know, a foot soldier here, a foot soldier there but I never mentioned you."

"That brings me to my next question. What did you tell them?"

Now Brooklyn and Chance were looking in his direction.

"Like I said, nothing really. They don't know nothing about you. Think about it, Rasim. If they did, do you think you'd be free right now?"

"It takes years to build a RICO case, mothafucka," Brooklyn added because he couldn't find credence in his eyes.

"I swear I don't know shit about that, Brooklyn," he said looking around Rasim to see him. If he did a good enough job, he figured he could call Rasim off. "The only thing I signed up for was a few low level cats who aren't worth nothing. They would've never been linked to you guys."

Since he denounced the dope game to save himself, Rasim lit a match and threw it. A shock wave of heat pushed toward Rasim, Brooklyn and Chance and they moved back. The flames missed their flesh by inches.

Vance screamed loudly as the inferno blanketed his body. Necklacing was one of the most torturous things that could be done to a human being and Rasim loved every bit of it.

It took fifteen minutes for Vance to die and Rasim didn't take his eyes off the blaze one time. The smell of burnt flesh did nothing but make him covet power.

When the show was over, Rasim turned around and faced Brooklyn and Chance. "Put the fire out and have somebody pick up the remains."

In the moment, he reminded his friends of Donald and they hoped he wouldn't suffer his same fate.

"Are you aight, man?" Brooklyn frowned after witnessed the crime.

A sly grin situated on Rasim's face. "Come on, homie. It's a little too late to ask me that now. Don't you think?"

Rasim positioned himself in the front of Minnesota Avenue with Selena who had her arms crossed over her chest in anger. He called earlier to talk to her but once again refused to meet anywhere private. "I see you standing over there with an attitude but you better hear what I'm saying."

She looked over his shoulders as if he weren't there. "I said I'm listening, Rasim. You don't have to talk to me like I'm a kid. I'm not one of your little dope boys, you know?"

She was as salty as a sweaty dick in a box of popcorn for many reasons. First and foremost, she didn't appreciate Snow getting out on her at their home awhile back when she slapped and punched her. But the real source of her annoyance was that after all this time, Rasim still refused to give her any more dick.

The man was mad!

He knew they should've been fucking by now.

She hoped that since they had a son it would rekindle his sexual appetite and they would explore each other again. She was wrong. Rasim never got over how Selena pulled off on Snow when she caught them at Hains Point, almost destroying his relationship in the process, and he never would.

"Do you remember what I said to you when we were on the bus a long time ago?"

He stepped away from her, snatched the Kufi off his head before slapping it back on and stepping up to her again. "Fuck are you talking about, Selena? Why you bringing up shit from when we were kids? Shit is serious now."

"Do you remember or not?" she frowned.

"No."

"I said that we would forever be connected. You didn't believe me then." She slid a thick strand of hair behind her ear. "But you do now." She said slyly. "Don't you?"

PRISON THRONE

Rasim stepped back and his eyes rolled up and he glanced at the darkening sky. He pinched his nose, crossed his arms over his chest and focused back on her. Basically he was doing all he could to prevent from snuffing out her life. "Selena, those memories are yours not mine. What I'm telling you is specific and related to our son. You cannot tell Stanley that I'm his father or I'm going inside for nothing."

"It's too late for that, Rasim," she snapped. "I had to tell him because of how you approached me the day you came to his job. He knows you're his father."

"Fuck!" Rasim yelled walking a few steps away before rushing back. He didn't want Stanley to know he was his father because in order for his plan to work, Rasim couldn't be associated with a known snitch.

"What's wrong with you?" she asked.

"What's wrong with me?" he repeated sarcastically. "Bitch, everything!" He placed his hands on her shoulders and squeezed. The only reason she was alive was because he didn't want to kill his son's mother. "Selena, I told you not to tell him so when were you going to tell me that you already did? Once I was inside?"

"I'm telling you now."

"Because of you, I'm gonna have to treat him like a third world nigga. He's not going to like it and you won't either."

She slapped his hands off and he backed up. "It won't be hard, Rasim Nami. Because he doesn't know you anyway." She stormed off switching the entire way.

"'Ole stupid ass bitch," he mumbled as he watched her stomp off.

He regretted the day he went home on a pass and fucked that skank and now it was too late.

BY T. STYLES

With Vance and Selena out of the way, it was time to thank Snow properly. For the next few days he and Snow indulged in blissful sex. The way they did when they were first married. Although the escapade was meant to put Snow at ease and to express how much Rasim cared for her, in the end it caused her to resent his decision to bounce even more.

On the day before Rasim was going to violate his probation, he and Snow were lying in bed. Her head rested on his left bicep while he stroked her silky skin.

"I'm going to miss you, Rasim," she whimpered kissing his chest before resting her head again. "So much."

"I hope so, baby," he chuckled to lighten the mood. "If not, I'm not doing my job right."

"I'm serious, Rasim. A year is a long time and for some reason I feel like you've been gone already. I know it's part my fault, because of the fighting we've been doing and all, but it doesn't stop it from hurting so bad. I'm not the kind of woman who can survive without her husband. I feel like I'm dying already."

He looked down at her, kissed her lips and squeezed her tighter. "I'm coming back to you, Snow. Just trust me." He knew what else he had to say but he was hesitating. "And when I do, I'm going to give you a child of your own."

Jackpot!

Snow hopped up, straddled Rasim and looked down at him with a wide smile to match her wide eyes. "Are you serious, Rasim?"

"I am," he exhaled. "I know this has been hard for you and that you sacrificed a lot. It's time for me to return the favor."

Snow thanked him as best she could, with a steamy fuck session. They made love the entire night until neither could cum anymore and she lay in his arms until the morning.

At sunrise, instead of it being a normal day, Rasim had work to do. He woke up, showered and sat at the kitchen table as Snow prepared a healthy plate of fried eggs, wheat toast and bacon. When his belly was jammed, he was given his first cool glass of Mimosa in a crystal flute.

He held it in his hand, looked up at Snow as she stood behind him, and then downed the entire glass in one gulp. Rasim hadn't drank in years but being wasted was a part of the plan. He needed to be fucked up when he sat in front of his parole officer.

Snow poured him glass after glass and his head wobbled around and he could barely hear.

After drinks were served, Snow sat across from him and rolled splif after splif at the kitchen table. When she was done he smoked all five blunts and she even joined him a few times. When the drunk and high session was concluded, Rasim lost complete control of his neck and the only thing he saw was the ceiling and the fan.

Now that he was blitzed, she assisted him into her car. Since he didn't have access to his limbs, he fell headfirst in and she pushed his legs and feet inside before closing the door and driving him to his parole officer.

When they arrived, she parked in front of the center. Tears rolled down her face and when she wiped them away, more followed. She wanted to be strong. That's what he demanded of her but he was hammered so she felt he wouldn't notice.

She rubbed his hair again and moved in for a kiss but he threw up in her mouth. She squinted while tasting the foulness of the champagne, eggs and meat and she opened the door and spit it out.

Shaking her head, she grabbed napkins from her glove compartment and cleaned him up the best she could.

"I'm sorry, baby," he responded with several bobbles of his head. "I think I did too much."

She giggled. "You think?" She wiped some creeping tears again. "You just make sure you come back to me, Rasim. Because for some reason, I feel like this is it between me and you."

"I don't give a fuck what happens in there, I will be back for my wife." He pushed the door open and toppled to the ground. It was the only time she ever saw her husband minus the grace. Eventually he made it to his feet and slammed the door so hard her eardrums rang.

She didn't help him this time. He was out of her hands. Instead she watched as he swerved toward the large glass door leading to the office.

Before long, he vanished inside.

CHAPTER 20

RASIM

CUMBERWOODS FEDERAL CORRECTIONAL INSTITUTION – MEDIUM

Face up, looking at the bunk above his head, Rasim wondered once again if he made a mistake. Successful at violating his parole, he was now forced to consider what lay before him. One hand rested in the back of his head and the other was tucked just under the belt line on his brown prison khakis.

He had been there for a week and still had not seen his son. Although he didn't have a bond with him yet, he didn't want him to get killed before he had a chance to save his life either. The love he held in his heart for Stanley was primitive of course. He was his son and at that moment it was nothing more or nothing less. The goal was to reshape his damaged mind due to Rasim missing the wonder years, so an event like this would not happen again.

Originally Rasim assumed that he would go directly into general population but the captain reviewed his sheet and considered him a high risk. After all, Rasim held dominion over the DC population and with a wave of his hand could cause an all out war.

So the captain kept him segregated pending an interview. The purpose was to reach into his mind in the hopes of seeing Rasim's position and motives. But Rasim put on a show worthy of an Emmy of course and now he was waiting on the verdict.

When Rasim's cell door opened, he sat up on the bunk. It was Officer House, a handsome fellow, with swelling muscles that threatened the threads of his uniform. House's motto was simple: follow the rules and you'll have enough respect from me to have an easier ride. "Let's go, Nami," the guard said. "You're being transferred to another cell."

Rasim stood from the bed, strolled up to the officer and turned around. Cool handcuffs were placed on his wrists and he was escorted to his new home.

When they arrived to his cell, he spun around and faced the bunk and Officer House removed the cuffs. After he organized his spot, it was showtime. He stepped to the mirror on the wall, adjusted his white Kufi and bounced out of the cell.

The moment he passed the first corridor, two inmates, Parker and Shawn, followed Rasim to protect him with their young lives. No orders had to be given either. Rasim was king and the moment they received the intel that he was arriving, they signed up for the duty. Rasim knew the young men's fathers who were both killed at one time or another while on the dope battlefield so he knew they came from the proper breed.

With each step of his boot against the grungy floor, men of lesser caliber felt their hearts stop. Moments earlier they were loud-mouthed fools looking to scare newborn punks who hadn't been in prison longer than a few months. But now that Rasim was on the block they avoided eye contact for fear he'd pull their cards. They wouldn't dare try that weak ass game on him.

Past the fakes, past the intimidated, he continued until he reached a pool of men of his stature. Men who were noble but due to a wrong move here or a glory killing there, before long, they earned the epithet of *Career Criminal.*

Rasim greeted the menfolk with firm handshakes and eye-to-eye contact. Although they were pleased to see their comrade, they didn't want him behind the wall. He was good people and they respected him.

Rasim had made each of them wealthy in and out of prison and they owed him their lives. They were Timothy, Whitaker and Eddie of southeast DC.

True gladiators.

"Aw shit, look at Hairy Monster," Timothy joked.

Rasim rubbed his growing beard. "You know what it is. I needed a change."

"Speaking of change, let's get to the question at hand," Timothy said as he crossed his arms over his chest. "What you doing back in this bitch?" Timothy was a large light-skinned male with hanging black moles over his face. They itched terribly and every now and again he'd scratch one off too roughly and it would bleed and topple to the floor. He was the last nigga you wanted around your food.

"It's a long story," Rasim said as he stood with his hands clutched before his body. Remembering he was in prison, despite his soldiers holding the line, he glanced around to assess his surroundings. "Let's just say I made a wrong move and now I'm back."

"I'm surprised they brought you here though," Timothy said. "This joint been so crowded they been tossing niggas out the window just for space."

"Well I can't say I want you in here either but I'm happy to see you well, homie," Whitaker interrupted as he clasped his hands behind him. Whitaker was tall and dark–skinned and wore a six-inch cicatrix across his face.

"So what's up, Ras? You still heavy on them weights?" Eddie questioned as he play boxed him from below. "'Cause you look like you grew a knot or two." He chuckled.

Eddie stood 5'5" if you were giving credit for how high his chin extended toward the air. If not, he was 5'2 with more wrinkles on his brown skin than what was normal for a man of twenty-two.

"How 'bout I show you instead," Rasim challenged, rubbing his hands together.

"Shit you ain't said nothing but a word."

The four good friends and Rasim's personal bodyguards hit it to the yard talking shit the whole way. Once outside, he scanned the environment for the one man he felt was worth a year of his life. Stanley. His only son. After a thorough stationary investigation, he spotted him standing next to Gordon who was lifting heavy. Gordon was lying on his back and sweat puddles rolled away from his face while watering the grass beneath him.

Stanley's hands were cupped in front of him. Head low. Eyes against the ground. When Rasim squinted he saw that his face was outlined with so many blue bruises that he looked as though he was ready for a casket.

Rasim didn't feel like lifting weights anymore.

PRISON THRONE

Upon seeing the condition of his son's face, Rasim's muscles bubbled all over his body like cooking popcorn in a bag.

Judging by the stiffness of Stanley's stance it was obvious what was going on. His man-child belonged to Gordon.

Rasim's forehead started sweating and his upper lip was glistening too. The urge to commit homicide was so strong he could see himself with a solid twenty if he made an imprecise move.

He closed his eyes and shook his head. He had to calm down because this wasn't the plan. Getting arrested for shaving Gordon's arteries would not help himself or Stanley in the least. But before he could activate his new plans, his comrades noticed the shift in his disposition.

"You aight?" Eddie asked touching his forearm with a firm grip. He was short but it didn't mean that he would avoid a battle or a fresh scar if Rasim deemed it necessary. Before receiving an answer, Eddie scanned the yard himself for a hometown villain who could've caused his friend such dismay.

"Naw, I'm cool," Rasim lied as he looked away from his son and pretended to be focusing on a band of Virginia niggas huddled in a group like a losing NFL team. "Just thinking about some shit that's all."

He dropped his hand. "Oh," Eddie responded in a relieved tone. "You know the rules, man. Once you in here, the outside world don't matter."

Rasim heard him but he was on some other shit. He knew if his next statement was related to Stanley in any way, then later that night, when his comrades were lying in their bunks going over the dailies, at least one of them would be perceptive enough to peep the father-son resemblance in spite of the hair that covered Rasim's face.

So he produced another conversation about this bad bitch he fucked five years ago that didn't exist. It worked too. If his homies loved nothing else, they were suckers for a good New Pussy Story.

Fifteen minutes later he figured he stalled enough. So he focused on Stanley again and asked, "Who the kid with the banged out face?" He pointed at him.

"Aww, that's some snitch from DC," Whitaker responded rubbing the scar on his face before allowing his hand to plop down. "He was involved in that church robbery that happened uptown not too long ago."

"Oh yeah?" Rasim responded with raised brows.

"Yeah," Timothy added as he took a moment to scratch around one of the larger moles on his face. "Young boy caught a case of bitch teeth and got a lesser sentence than his homies. But them niggas got shipped out Philly somewhere, I think." Timothy looked at Stanley with disgust. He hated lip flappers. "Gordon bitch ass be having that snitch doing all kinds of shit too. Cleaning his room, buying stuff from the commissary using his account and everything. I even saw him brushing the nigga's teeth one day." He shook his head. "It's pitiful but the boy had it coming."

The moment the last statement rotated off of Timothy's lips, Stanley disobeyed Gordon's rule and looked up to stretch his neck because it caught a cramp and hurt something terrible. When he saw his father standing in the yard, he grew goggle-eyed, released his cupped hands and bounced confidently in Rasim's direction.

"Hold up, what type shit the young boy on?" Eddie said as he peeped the lad's course, which was headed their way.

Parker and Shawn stepped in front of Rasim, eager to slap him back into the head lowered, eyes down, immobile stance he was known for all day. Eddie grabbed the hidden shank with intentions to slice.

But the moment Stanley was in front of them in preparation to speak, Rasim stepped up and stole him in the face so hard that he fractured the lower level of his jaw.

His only child passed out cold.

CHAPTER 21

SNOW

Snow was driving down the highway with more shit on her mind than her heart could hold. Her hands shook as she steered the car on the way to see her husband. It had been three whole weeks since she laid eyes on him. And for a bitch like Snow who moved based on her nigga's heartbeat, the separation was pushing her toward the brink of insanity.

When she saw a traffic accident up ahead her eyes popped open and she clutched the steering wheel tighter. Apparently a black Honda thought it could give a red Porsche some competition and found itself in the family way...pregnant with a guardrail stuck under its body. Meanwhile the driver of the Porsche was already clocked in at work.

Snow sighed because she knew the hour was approaching for visitation to be over and if the traffic jam didn't vanish soon, she wouldn't be able to see her love until next week. Truthfully she was supposed to already be there but one of their mules got arrested in the middle of the night and Snow had to make provisions. She hadn't had a moment's sleep.

When her cell phone rang she gripped the purse in her seat and wrestled with the lotion, mirror and Victoria Secret's catalogue all while her eyes remained on the road. When she felt the coolness of the phone in her palm she snatched it, turned it on and pressed it against her ear so hard air got trapped in her drum and she had to release it and reapply just to hear.

Due to the traffic jam, she couldn't move any further. So after listening to the greeting and accepting the option to speak to Rasim, she waited to hear his voice.

The first thing she heard was huffing and puffing.

She could tell by the way his agitated breath pushed into the phone that he wasn't in a cheery mood. "Where the fuck you at?"

She swallowed and looked at the pregnant Honda, which was just being separated from its baby. The guard-rail. "Behind a traffic accident. I'm coming as soon as I can, baby."

Rasim's breaths grew heavier, causing Snow's intestines to roll like a belly dancer.

"Why you didn't leave earlier, Snow? Huh? You didn't want to see me? You fucking up already and it ain't even been a month yet? Huh? Tell me now!"

Of course she couldn't tell him what happened over the phone. She needed to wait until she saw him to give him the details.

Rasim was no stranger to the penitentiary system and Snow was no stranger to holding him down. But something else was up. She was shocked at the tone of his voice and it didn't feel right. Was he guilty of something that she was unaware of?

During the other stints, he appreciated how hard she worked for him and told her in letters, calls and visits. But now he was short and it was as if he were trying to pick an argument on purpose. "You know I want to see you," she said softly as she tried to release the urge to cry. "I haven't been able to sleep since I haven't been in your arms. I'm dying here, husband."

"Then act like it, Snow! And get up here before I go the fuck off." He hung up.

Snow made one more attempt to prevent her tears from falling but it was useless so she allowed them to roll. At one point she was crying so hard that she couldn't see that the traffic jam cleared and allowed her a pass until she was honked out by the tractor trailer behind her. She cleared her vision by using her knuckles and pushed forward.

Lately Rasim was sure proving to be unreasonable. At first it started with him suggesting that she refrain from making a move in the morning until she received his call. A few days later his suggestions turned into demands and he added that she had better create an email account and be accessible there too. His possession reached all time heights and it was harder to juggle him now than it was when he was home.

With the threat of Rasim's words still fresh on her mind, she hit it to the prison at lightning speeds. She removed her heel so that her foot could cover the gas pedal and she stomped on that like an expert drum major. Once Snow seriously applied herself, she was at the prison in thirty minutes flat before Visitor Registration was over.

Sweating, with her heartbeat pounding against the walls of her chest, she threw herself on the counter and scribbled her name on the sign in sheet.

Mindy, a fat correctional officer who hadn't had dick since one of the inmates rubbed it against her inner jaw, for five dollars at that, grew heated when she saw her last name. There wasn't a bitch in Cumberwoods or out of it that didn't want Rasim. Why did she get to have him?

PRISON THRONE

However, she and Snow had another mutual friend and her name was Queen. She was paid to do a job and had plans to be the best hater within her ability.

Stuffing her fists into her hips, she leaned back and scanned Snow up and down. She knew there was no way she would allow Rasim this visit and her only other duty was to find the proper reason why.

She looked at Snow's shoes and they met code. She observed the blue jeans and they met code too. She thought all was lost until she saw the cream top she wore. Although a C.O. with good intentions would've allowed Snow in anyway, because you really couldn't see a thing, Mindy was anything but honorable.

She rubbed the whiskers sprouting on her chin and said, "You got another shirt, right?"

Snow looked down at her blouse, which was not revealing in the least. "No," she said softly. "What's wrong with—"

"You ain't coming in here with that," she said shaking her head so hard she stumbled backwards due to getting dizzy. "You can't be wearing nothing like that up in here. I'm sorry." She shook her head some more. "If I let you in, I got to let other people in too and I'm not having that in my prison." Feeling unbalanced, she flopped down in the rolling chair.

"Let the girl go, Mindy," Courtney said looking down at her coworker.

Courtney was also a C.O. and whenever the inmates saw her face, they knew it would be a cool day because she respected the men despite the things they had done. She was a prime example that not every officer had ill motives, but it was the ones who did that fucked up the party.

BY T. STYLES

Courtney wanted the inmates to see their family members, knowing that without support they would go mad and then that could be trouble for all.

Mindy, angry that Courtney's happy-go-lucky ass was stunting her groove, leaped up and said, "Wait a minute, I don't come bothering you when you're doing your job so don't come for me when I'm doing mine." She was wagging her finger like a happy dog's tail a little too closely to Courtney's face. "I'm not having any of that in my prison. No sir-ree."

Courtney glared at the mean spirited woman because although she was easygoing, she still reserved the right to rise on a bitch or two. "Ain't nobody telling you not to do your job. But the man hasn't seen his wife since—"

"How you figure?" she frowned. "His wife was up here last week," Mindy advised trying to stir up the pot, which was already boiling over with shit. "So mind your business. Please and thank you," she said sarcastically.

When Snow heard that his wife had been up there last week, she thought she was watching someone else's life. The top of her forehead tightened and her nose burned. The sensation spread itself downward to her chest and it felt like someone was crushing her heart. "Excuse me," Snow whispered, "did you say that...that his wife came up here already?"

Courtney, knowing the deal, shook her head and walked away. She tried to save Snow but Mindy opened a dumpster full of mess and she left her to clean it up.

"Look, I don't get involved in inmate affairs," she said rolling her eyes. "I'm just letting you know that you not getting in here with that shirt." She shook her head again. "No sir-ree, you not coming up in my prison with that shit on." With that, the hating ass bitch strutted toward the back shaking her head the entire way.

Defeated, Snow turned around, pushed the glass door open and took the walk of Denied Visitor Shame. When she made it to the parking lot, and then her car, she allowed the gallons of tears she held to flow freely. Otherwise it would have been impossible to drive the full four hours home.

What did Mindy mean by his wife came last week? Snow wanted answers and she wanted them now.

She was about to pull off when Rasim rang. She put the car in park again and waited for the greeting to select the proper keys and accept the call. The moment she did, Rasim yelled, "Where the fuck—,"

"Did you have a bitch up here last week, Rasim?" she snatched the mic from that nigga. "Because if Selena coming up here to see you, I'm done this time! I'm not fucking playing!" Snow was on fire and it felt good unloading on his ass. That is until she heard, click.

She overplayed her hand.

"Hello...hello." She looked at her cell phone and saw the call was ended.

In all of the years she'd known or been married to Rasim, he never hung up on her before now. She was so devastated that her lips trembled like knocking cymbals and she lost her appetite.

She didn't want to fight with Rasim. She wasn't about that life. All she wanted was to be there for her husband and support him in his journey. Didn't he see that? Couldn't he feel her love?

Somehow Snow pulled herself out of the parking lot and took the long drive home.

The next morning she was lying in bed, on her side looking at the wall. Her head throbbed so bad it was hard to move. Would Rasim call her back? Would he send her an email? The answer was unequivocally no.

For two whole days he avoided all contact with her, sending her emotions on a frenzy. He didn't even call to ask about business. Thinking something must be wrong, she reached out to his counselor, Joanne Franklin, and discovered he was not locked down or in trouble. She hung up before asking if he was sick so she got back on the horn and called the infirmary but he wasn't there either.

It was obvious what was going on. He was sitting on his prison throne, probably eating smuggled in outside food and ignoring her purposely. But why? Was she that bad of a wife to deserve the isolation? To be frozen out of his love? When he knew how much she loved him?

She decided to write him a letter.

Dear Rasim,
I have been reflecting on our lives together. We've been in love since we were kids. I want you to know I have your back always. And although we haven't been doing too good with our love, I know things will get better.

She wrote a few more lines and then folded it up. When she mailed the letter she went back into the house to quarantine herself. It had been a week since she heard from her husband and approaching two.

In the beginning she would give Mute Candy the benefit of sending a text saying that she was fine. But when another week passed and she didn't see her friend's face or text, Mute Candy broke into the house.

PRISON THRONE

Snow was lying in the floor in front of the TV, balled up in a comforter when she found her. Mute Candy cleaned Snow's pussy since it was obvious by the way she smelled that she did not. The girls got her dressed, fed her and they all pulled her into the sunlight. For the first hour Snow was too devastated to talk but during the second hour she bawled her eyes out.

Since they were in the car when the mental explosion occurred, Mute Candy rubbed her leg and each twin rubbed a shoulder in an expression of love. Although they knew the pain she was having could only be repaired with the return of Rasim, they would not allow her to fall into the abyss without at least giving it a try.

Three hours later, the twins and Mute Candy had hugged her so much Snow couldn't do anything but smile. She was still devastated but she refused to tell Mute Candy what Rasim was doing. She knew she would be back with her husband and hated the tension her best friend and man would have during the rough times.

The only thing was that Mute Candy was far from dumb. It didn't take long for her to analyze the situation but she didn't burden her with her opinions either.

A bitch was involved.

Point. Blank. Period.

Instead of pushing the issue, she and the twins took Snow to get her toes and nails done and then they went to the Cheesecake Factory for a few stiff drinks. When Snow was grinning and holding regular conversation, Mute Candy felt she was good.

With Snow all loved up and feeling better, she returned her home. And that's when her nigga called.

She was sitting on the edge of the bed removing her shoes when she answered her cell. "Hello."

"Snow," he said softly. At first she thought she was dreaming because she didn't hear the Cumberwoods greeting. But when he said, "Are you there?" she knew it was her man. He had a cell phone inside the walls.

What was a king without his spoils?

"Y-yes," she stuttered.

"What you been doing?"

She responded by crying so hard he barely knew what she said. She missed him so much that hearing his voice stimulated her soul and caused a torrent of emotions. "Where...where...where have you...you been?" she managed while hiccupping in the process. "I wanted to die, Rasim. Why would you do this to me? Are you trying to kill me?"

"I'm here. Where else would I be?" He sounded so cold and unsympathetic it was horrible. In the past he could never face her crying and would work overtime to make her feel better. In this situation, he didn't apply himself at all.

"Did I do something wrong? If I did, is it something I can do to make things better?"

"You checking on stuff?" he asked referring to the business in code words.

"Yes...I am...of course," she responded as she rolled herself into a ball on the edge of the bed.

In one phone call, Rasim had undone all of Mute Candy's work.

"You know I wouldn't let you down like that." She looked at a space on the wall, between the door and her dresser.

"I can't tell. Lately you been weak. I thought you would hold me down, Snow? I thought you would ride for me while I was in here. You lying to me now?"

"I thought I was. If I'm not, I'm so sorry. Rasim, please tell me what I'm doing wrong and I will correct it instantly. I'm begging you."

"You gonna come next weekend?"

Snow wanted to but she was horrified. She could tell by Mindy's vibe that she didn't fuck with her and getting rejected in front of an entire prison was humiliating. What if she attempted another visit and she couldn't get in? Would Rasim take that out on her too? "I'll try hard, Rasim. I promise. But I don't think the C.O. likes me."

"Try harder," he said before hanging up.

True to her word, Snow got herself dressed in the baggiest clothing she owned when it was visit time. Although Snow didn't have much of an ass she did make up for it in the boob department and worked overtime to hide her titty blessings.

Since her clothing was horrible because they didn't expose any of her curves, she fixed up her hair and makeup really pretty. And it worked too. She was gorgeous despite her gear and she hoped she would look good enough for Rasim.

When she felt presentable, she dragged herself out of the house and to the car. As she steered down the highway, she quivered the closer she got to the prison. To an outsider, it would appear that Snow was making too much of the matter. But Rasim was her everything and she hated when they quarreled. If she couldn't see him this time, she knew it wouldn't be good for her marriage.

So she thought it was time to call for reinforcements.

This time it wouldn't be Mute Candy.

She needed God.

"God, I know lately our conversations are few and far between. And I know that I haven't been one of Your favorite people. But I know You are a forgiving God. And I know You know that everything I do is out of love for my husband. Whether good or bad, I am honoring Your word. Colossians 3:18 says, 'Wives, submit to your husbands, as it is fitting to the Lord'. So please, God, please let me see my husband today if it be Your will. And only if it be Your will. Amen."

When she made it to the prison, she was the first one inside and her heart rejoiced when she saw Courtney, the nicer C.O., standing behind the counter. But what she didn't realize was that the devil had a full time job. While Snow was approaching the sign in sheet, Ole' Hating Ass Mindy was preparing a fake calamity as she wrote.

Mindy grabbed the intercom, pressed it against her dry lips and said, "Officer Doughty, you're needed in Cell Block 4! Officer Doughty, you're needed in Cell Block 4!"

When Courtney ignored the call to assist Snow with her visit, as quickly as possible, the hater grew desperate. "Officer Doughty, I'll help the visitor," she said with an attitude over the speakers. "Go now and see what they want! I will help the visitor!" She was doing a little more than what needed to be done on the intercom but haters were always extra.

Not trying to ignore a call, thereby losing her job, Courtney stopped the sign in process and looked at Snow with sad eyes. "I'm sorry. I really am. I tried, sweetheart."

Courtney knew what was about to go down. Snow would not be seeing her husband today or any other day if Mindy had anything to do with it. Reluctantly Courtney proceeded to Cell Block 4 with her head hung low in recognition of Snow's pain.

True to her hating game, Mindy crawled from the back and looked Snow up and down. She was shaking her head so hard she was getting dizzy but this time she would not sit down. She wanted to remain planted for this bitch.

Truthfully it didn't matter what piece of clothing Snow wore. Both of them knew it. So Mindy stabbed her dark fists into her hips and said, "You not getting in with that on." She pointed at her body.

"With what on?" Snow asked in a low voice knowing the war was already lost.

"With everything on. I can't have all of that up in my prison! No, sir-ree! Now get out of here. Visit denied."

"Please, Officer, all I want to do is—"

"Excuse me," she yelled throwing her hand up in Snow's face. Her fingers were so close to her nose that she could smell the chocolate cookie she gulped down seconds earlier. "I said I'm not having all of that up in here. You're dismissed! Please and thank you."

Snow's head lowered as she examined the clothes that covered her body. She could not have found a looser outfit if she wore a plastic bag. Defeated, she turned around with her beating heart in her hands. Snow Nami didn't like that feeling. Now that she thought about it, she didn't like the shit at all.

It was a full moon later that night when Mindy was getting off of work. And a few wolves from southeast DC were waiting in the parking lot, eager to tear her apart. Hard hitting bitches with zero love in their hearts for officers of the law, they whipped Mindy so bad her uniform tore off. All in the name of Snow.

Because Mindy was a career hater since birth and had wronged so many, she was clueless on whom to blame. But she would have three weeks in a hospital room while nursing a cracked forehead, a fractured collarbone and two broken legs to consider possible motives.

BY T. STYLES

When Snow made it home after the attempted visit, she waited for Rasim's call. She felt like a student waiting on her parents after receiving all D's on her report card. For some reason she figured it wouldn't end well.

In the past he blew up her phone immediately pending a failed visit but this time was different. Why? Rasim didn't hit his beautiful wife until 7pm that evening and every second, every single minute, was pure torture.

"So you don't know how to dress now, huh?"

Snow couldn't believe her ears. As if he didn't know what he meant to her, he chose to berate her on the phone like some bum bitch.

Instead of losing it again, Snow went back in her mind to the prayer she made before going to the prison. She asked if it be God's will to let her see him. Perhaps it wasn't, because she didn't get in.

Without a word more, Snow slammed the phone down in his ear. Angry about everything she experienced, she decided it was time to clean up her house and her life. She'd deal with her husband tomorrow.

In the past, a thorough cleaning always got her mind off of her troubles and it was time to return to the basics. So Snow spun around the living room, kitchen and bathroom so well that you could eat or fuck on the floors.

Rasim called like he was crazy but she refused to answer the phone.

When she was done in the house, she went outside to sweep the porch. One house over on the left, Old Lady Bridget was sitting in her chair rocking and frowning as usual. She still didn't like the young couple, believing they were terrorists, and nothing would change but her wigs. In fact her brown skin earned a new wrinkle every time she came outside and saw one of their faces.

Snow ignored the bitch. Besides, she had gripes of
her own. She continued to busy herself with her chores until a truck with the words KING AMONGST KINGS Auto
Body Shop strolled up in front of her house. A pretty fat
chick with rosy cheeks rolled the window down and said,
"'Scuse me, but is Rasim in there?"

Snow thought she was hearing things. She stopped
sweeping and tried to see if she recognized the black woman's face. She didn't. Frowning, she asked, "What you doing calling on my husband?"

The girl grinned and said, "Never mind, forget I even
came by." She turned the radio up and pulled off.

Snow started to consider the possible reasons the girl
would pull up to her house. She figured it must've been a
bitch with a soft crush because over the last six months
Rasim received a lot of bodywork for his truck.

Now that she thought about it, every time she turned
around his truck was in the shop and she didn't understand
why. Rasim always took great care of his vehicles and
maintained maintenances from the time they crawled off of
the showroom floor to the moment he sold them and
bought another. So he shouldn't have needed that much
work.

But the girl, although pretty, was not his body type.
So she shrugged and walked back in the house to wash
clothes. The whites were in the wash and she was preparing the pile of dark clothes when she dipped into pocket
after pocket until she felt something folded in a pair
Rasim's jeans.

Slowly she pulled it out and saw the words KING
AMONGST KINGS Auto Body Shop scrawled on the
front. The contact person's name was Queen Dower.

Snow's jaw dropped in disbelief.

Well she never saw that bitch coming.

Queen hustled about her auto body shop after a very profitable weekend. The tight black jeans she wore along with the red low-cut top presented the perfect amount of whore necessary to lure some of the more profitable hustlers to purchase expensive tires and rims.

After seeing Rasim two days back to back, for two weekends in a row, thanks to Mindy running interference, Queen was certain that when he was released he would leap into her arms like a pitbull puppy fresh out the cage.

Queen flung her long brown hair over her shoulder and was all smiles and giggles until the bell rang indicating another customer entered her place of business. Within a moment's time, she was staring into the beautiful big brown eyes of Mrs. Rasim Nami.

Queen had pushed Snow into a corner and now she was ready to attack.

Queen's eyelids fluttered rapidly in several attempts to change the view but to no avail. Fifty flaps later, Snow was still staring calmly in her direction.

She raised the creased business card Queen left in her husband's pocket and said, "You rang?"

Queen knew the card would cause trouble but she wasn't prepared for the aftermath. Had she considered the possibility that Snow had transformed into a bold bitch, she would've created a plan. Instead of dealing with the matter at hand, Queen shuffled papers around on the counter as if she were trying to locate her lines. When all seemed lost, she sighed and said, "You can sit over there." She pointed to the left. "I have to help my customers first and then I'll be right with you."

Snow swaggered to one of the large king's thrones as if she were wearing a cloak, took a seat, crossed her legs and patiently waited.

Hoping to test her patience and force Snow to leave, Queen did all she could to stall. At first she helped people who she already assisted, then she took to doing her cashier's job by taking phone calls and order requests. And then it got extra weird when she completed the janitor's duties and took to cleaning the break room.

But when all of the antics were over, when the performance was done, Mrs. Rasim Nami was still waiting, wearing a smile as cool as an afternoon Jamaican breeze.

It was time.

Queen knew it.

So she had better muscle up.

Slowly Queen strutted around the counter and toward the throne next to Snow and said, "Long time no see."

Snow nodded but preferred to get straight down to business. "So you're fucking my husband?"

Queen's tongue flitted around like a butterfly before landing safely at the bottom of her mouth. "I don't know what you're talking about."

Snow sat back in the chair and ran her hands down the sides of her thighs before clasping them in her lap. The diamond ring she wore was larger than a bag of convict knuckles and shined so brightly Queen titled her head slightly to remove the shine out of her eyes.

Snow was angry, hurt and embarrassed but that's not the impression Queen received. Snow smiled as if she could care-the-fuck-less what the tart did with her husband. In fact, a few of her employees, who huddled in front of the store as if everything that needed to be done existed out front, assumed the two of them were best good girlfriends Snow was grinning so wide.

"You left me a message, Queen," Snow said wiggling her foot. "You even sent your truck to my home. Now if you are fucking Rasim, and I assume that you are, what the fuck do you want with me?" She smiled brighter. "Be a woman, shawty. I'm here."

Snow was tougher than the heels of a barefoot islander. And there was no use in lying and Queen knew it. "You are correct. I am fucking Rasim."

Snow was gut punched. Although she already knew it was true, hearing it was a whole 'nother animal. She smelled a woman on him a long time ago but in her haste she assumed it was Selena. In all of those torturous days she never thought that Rasim would return to the sea to pick another fish. "So if you're fucking Rasim, what do you hope to gain by contacting me? Why not just do you, boo-boo?"

"I want the prize."

"Being?"

"Rasim."

Snow shook her head and laughed. "You will never get my husband," she assured her with soft headshakes. "Not in the way you want him at least. You were a sexual exploit, honey. He desired a ride and you provided your pussy for his amusement and pleasure. But now, well now, sweetheart, I'm afraid the carnival is over."

Queen frowned and whipped her hair over her shoulder in nervousness. "He wasn't saying that when he ate my pussy," she said slyly. "As a matter of fact every time you kissed him, you were licking me...just...like...Rasim." She was feeling herself now. She even took to brushing imaginary lint off of her shoulder blades as if she'd already won a prized fight.

"You waited a long time to use that phrase, didn't you?" Snow giggled. "I'm talking about the licking your pussy thing."

Amazing!

Snow was correct.

Queen studied those lines in the mirror obsessively. Except, in the screenplay she wrote it was said when Snow came to her and Rasim's home begging him to take her back. But now she was embarrassed that her words didn't hold much weight.

Why was Snow Nami smiling instead of crying?

"You're absolutely right," Snow conceded. "Every time I peck his lips I'm probably tasting remnants of you." She paused trying to force her tears back with an even brighter smile. She would not give the bitch the satisfaction of seeing her fall on her sword. "But tell me something. Was it good?"

"Spectacular."

Snow nodded. "That's dope." She paused. "That's real dope. But where do you think he got his technique?" Snow pointed at herself. "Because I guarantee you that you, my dear, have tasted way more of my juicy pussy than I ever have of yours." She touched Queen's leg with three fingers. "Understand something, sweetheart. Without the benefit of my love, Rasim is as worthless in life as my jeans." Snow sat back and grinned.

"Meaning?" Queen said sarcastically.

Instead of verbalizing her point Snow elected to give old girl a visual. She stood up, wiggled out of her jeans and released them to the floor. With that, she sat back on the throne. Everybody in the shop admired the tattoo artwork on her leg, particularly the way RASIM appeared to crawl down her pretty yellow thigh.

Shit, even Queen was in awe.

It's funny. Before meeting The New and Improved Snow, she could never see how such a soft-spoken woman could hold such a strong man. Now she understood. He had made her into his image and his work was great.

"Without the warmth of my body, Rasim does not move, just like my jeans. So you see, sweetie, instead of disrespecting you should be on your knees and praising the true Queen."

Queen bit at the inside of her bottom lip. "He wants to be with me," Queen muttered with a quivering jaw.

"He didn't tell you that," Snow said confidently. Although he cheated she would bet what remained of her heart that her husband would never go to those lengths for her twat. "The nigga was about to die before I returned myself to him. I am his savior, Queen. Not you."

Queen smirked and leaned back in the seat and crossed her legs. "We'll see about that."

Suddenly things had gotten interesting. Snow reclined and observed Queen closely. She peeped the way Queen's chin was pulled so high that she had a clear view of her inner nostrils. She observed the way Queen's shoulders stretched from side to side as if she were wearing a football player's shoulder pads. Snow laughed lightly and said, "Wait a minute." She pointed at her. "You think you got the juice."

"What?" Queen asked, never having seen the movie *Juice* before.

Snow waved her off with a toss of her hand. Her lack of movie knowledge was annoying at best.

"It doesn't even matter." Snow paused. "You know what, originally I was going to come in here, yank you outside by your hair and deposit you in several trash bags in my trunk." She continued to read Queen before she pointed at the window to her left.

Queen rocked in her seat when she saw the entrance lined with hood soldiers who made it obvious by the way their thumbs hung on their belts that they were strapped and ready for Snow to utter, "Attack."

When Snow could smell the fear, she snapped her fingers so that Queen was focusing back on her where the attention rightfully belonged. Besides, those men would not make a move without her command. "But now that I've spoken to you, I think I'll teach you a lesson instead."

Queen didn't feel so bold anymore. It was clear who had the juice and it damn sure wasn't her. "What about Rasim?" Queen whispered.

"To give you a head start in your futile attempt to steal my husband, I will keep this little meeting a secret from Rasim. Because if I ever told him that you stepped to me, you would be wearing a smile a bit wider on that stupid face, along with a burning tire around that snake-like neck of yours." As Snow parlayed with Queen, her phone rang in her purse. She picked it up and reviewed the caller. "What do you know?" She maneuvered the phone so that Queen could see the screen clearly. "He's calling me already." She tossed it into her purse, removed her wedding ring and threw it in Queen's lap. "I'm going to show Rasim what happens when my love is no longer available. And you will bear witness."

CHAPTER 22

RASIM

Rasim had been shitting nonstop ever since he first tried to reach Snow a week ago and was unsuccessful. He sent emails. He called obsessively. He even sent Backward Jake to the house to check on things since, outside of Brooklyn and Chance, who were out of town, he was the only person he trusted. After awhile it became obvious that either Snow was ignoring him on purpose or something else was terribly wrong.

Rasim couldn't get a wink of sleep since she disappeared. He was beside himself with worry. Prison was the last place a man with troubles needed to be. The mind had nothing to do all day but think of the worst case scenarios and Rasim had considered them all.

At the end of the day, Rasim had one question. Where was his wife? Where was his precious Snow?

Yes, something was definitely up. At first he thought it was Queen but he knew for a fact that Snow would've stepped to him if she found out about her. At least he hoped. Plus, Queen would never play with her life in that way. There were very few things in the world he toyed with and Snow Nami was not one of them. He expressed that to Queen...fiercely.

Besides, Queen already had a husband and he was certain that she didn't look at him in a long-term type of way. He was smart enough to know that. She even told him that when they spoke recently on the phone.

But if all that were true, and if all that could be said, why wasn't Snow answering the phone? If she was trying to get him back for treating her badly, it certainly worked.

Game over.

After his stomach grumbled, he looked at his son who was cleaning his shoes on the floor. Stanley's mouth was wired due to his jaw being fractured but unlike when he was with his friends, he didn't flap his gums to the powers that be. He took the face crunch like a G and remained silent. Stanley finally realized that talking too much had gotten him in enough trouble to last a lifetime. If nothing else, he learned a firm lesson.

Rasim couldn't believe he had given up a year of his life for this kid. He wasn't even sure if he was worth it. All he could do was hope so.

Instead of telling people that Stanley was his son, Rasim announced that he would make him his slave, thereby stealing him from Gordon. When asked why, Rasim said that Stanley approached a king without permission and servitude was the punishment.

Gordon didn't like the situation one bit when he learned that Rasim stole his golden boy. You have to understand. Selena kept Stanley's commissary stacked and since nobody outside of the prison fucked with Gordon, he had gotten used to the fringe benefits. Essentially Rasim reduced him to broke nigga status in one day flat. But what could he do? Step to Rasim, get stole in the face and risk being cross-eyed for the rest of his life? No. It simply wasn't worth it and Gordon knew it.

Rasim was lying on the bed trying to hold his bowel movement when he thought again about his missing wife.

His asshole already burned due to defecating constantly and he could no longer take the pain.

He was already having a shitty day, literally, when Montana Scissor Hands from uptown approached the door. He gained the nickname because he had successfully killed two people that the government knew about by way of slicing their throats. But there were many more lining the Chesapeake Bay.

When he tried to gain entrance into Rasim's cell he was stopped by a soft nudge to the chest by Shawn and Parker who remained on guard, only taking breaks to shit and sleep.

Rasim looked at who was visiting and reluctantly said, "Let him in." He didn't want to see anybody unless the person had hazel eyes and her last name was Nami but in jail he had to deal with niggas with stinky feet.

Irritated that the young boys laid hands on him, Montana brushed his chest, mugged them both and bopped inside of the cell. His arrogance was legendary and he made plans to show them later.

Rasim stood up and gave him the universal black man handshake. Clearly at this point folks forgot that he was Pakistani.

Rasim adjusted his Kufi and flopped back on the bottom bunk. His old cellmate received a pardon so he had the cell to himself. He was working on having Stanley moved into his room so he could keep a better eye on him but that would take a month to work out.

When Montana saw Stanley on the floor he frowned. "You still got this bitch ass nigga taking up your breathing space?" Montana was intent on bothering Stanley who was cleaning shoes and minding his own business.

PRISON THRONE

"He aight," Rasim said, not feeling like witnessing another attack on his child.

Besides, the other prisoners had gotten so vicious with Stanley that Rasim took to staying in his room with him just to keep him alive. It didn't make any sense because every time Stanley asked if he was his father on a sheet of paper, because he couldn't talk, Rasim said no. Although it was clear that he was protecting him. Not only that but Selena told him Rasim was his dad.

"He ain't aight to me," Montana glared. Out of odium, he plucked Stanley's head so hard it pierced the flesh and bled through his scalp.

When Rasim saw blood, he jumped in his face as visions of body blows danced in his head. When he remembered to keep the lie alive, he calmed down and said, "I said leave the little nigga alone, man. He cleaning my shit now." He sat back down and clasped his hands in front of him. "Now what can I do for you?"

Stanley rubbed the top of his head and felt the blood. It was no use in crying. Rasim told him that if he saw him crying again, he would pop his eyes out and send them to his mother. Stanley believed him too. So he picked up the shoe and handled his business.

Montana thought Rasim was a little overprotective of the snitch but to each convict his own. He shrugged and said, "I'm here 'bout Snow."

Rasim rose again but this time he would remain standing. His nostrils flared wildly as he waited for clarification. "What about her, nigga?"

Montana was shook. Where was the southern hospitality Rasim had given him moments earlier? "Ya'll...ya'll still married?"

BY T. STYLES

Rasim stepped closer and Montana didn't realize it yet but Parker and Shawn were already in the room ready to move something. They stood directly behind him.

"Why you ask me some shit like that?" Rasim huffed and puffed.

"Oh...I...'cause I thought ya'll weren't together. Since I see you with the broad Queen and all."

Dude was disrespecting on so many levels. "Let me tell you something," he stepped closer, "even if I choked her with my bare hands, and snuffed out her life, she would still be my wife. And I had better not find out that nobody touched her and that includes the pallbearer."

Oh shit! Montana thought.

It wasn't until that moment that Montana remembered that he and Rasim were not equals. Unfortunately he allowed the routine activities they shared as prisoners to cloud his judgment and now it was too late.

He swallowed. "Uh, it's just that...you know...my man said they saw her smiling in the grocery store with some dude the other day. So I was coming to ask you if you knew about that shit."

Montana would have been better off prison shanking Rasim because it would have the same effect for his life. Death.

Rasim's guts rocked even more and he placed his hand on his stomach in the hopes of calming them down. He felt dead. Light on his feet. Like he was no longer of that life.

With the one sentence that Montana spit, Rasim took to imagining Snow in a thousand compromising sexual positions. He imagined her getting fucked from the back, sucking another nigga's dick and even holding the baby she always wanted in her arms. He even saw its face, a beautiful little girl with eyes as big and as pretty as her mother's.

Then it got weird when he envisioned her removing the tattoo on her body with his name.

When Montana saw how angry he made the sleeping beast, he looked behind him for the exit but it was futile. Parker and Shawn were steady and already cracking their knuckles. Now that Montana had the proper script in hand and realized he wasn't running shit, he was aware that the only way he was leaving that cell was bleeding.

"So I guess ya'll niggas believe in shooting the messenger?" He tried to joke around.

The crowd was tough.

Nobody even chuckled.

When he focused back on Rasim he was staring into the eyes of a killer.

Angry that Montana assumed that they were cool enough for him to discuss his wife, Rasim rocked the nigga's chest plate until he was fifty shades of red. When he wanted a break, Shawn kicked him repeatedly in the chin while Parker took to mopping him on the floor.

Even Stanley got himself a free kick in, although he pretended as if it was because Montana was in his way.

The entire ordeal took less than two minutes and when Rasim was sure the coast was clear, they released Montana. Amazingly, he was able to walk out of Rasim's cell alive and in a daze. But the next morning when it was time for roll call he would be found dead in his sleep.

Rasim was on the yard with his son who decided that today was the day that he would talk to the man he believed was his father. The wire holding his jaw in place was removed and he was ready to use his lips. Not for snitching of course.

Shawn and Parker remained on guard, more perceptive than ever. It was quite unnecessary though because in the short time Rasim had been in prison one man received a fractured jaw and became his personal bitch, and the other died due to bleeding on the brain.

Wasn't nobody trying to fuck with Rasim. He carried his legend inside with him and had activated it even though it wasn't his plan.

Rasim was standing in the yard with an evil glare. Slowly Stanley raised his head and said, "I'm sorry about your wife."

Rasim was about to crunch his jaw again until he looked to the right and realized he was staring into his own face...he was staring at his son. "Thank you," he said under his breath.

Truthfully, with Snow gone he didn't think he could do a year. Had he thought he would lose his wife, he would've never stepped a foot inside of that bitch. At least that's what he told himself. He even wrote a letter questioning her about the nigga at the grocery store but she never responded.

"Can I talk to you? In private?" Stanley asked boldly.

There wasn't shit going on in the yard so Rasim adjusted the Kufi on his head, rubbed his beard and said, "Come on."

The four of them strutted to his cell as if on a mission. Parker and Shawn remained on the outside while Rasim and his son stayed inside.

Rasim flopped on the bottom bunk and clasped his hands in front of him as he looked up at him and waited for his question.

"Why don't you want to be my father?" Stanley uttered. "I know you are my dad. I knew from the time I first saw your face. And my mama told me too."

Rasim hopped up and got so close to Stanley that Stanley could smell the remnants of the meat Rasim had for breakfast. He stabbed a stiff finger in his chest so hard it throbbed. "I told you once but I'm not going to tell you again," he spoke through clenched teeth. "I am not your fucking father. If you say it again...just once more...the way I feel right now, I will hurt you."

"But your face...you look li—"

"What the fuck is wrong with you?" Rasim screamed in his face, splashing him with spit crystals. "Didn't you hear what I just said, lil nigga? I said I'm not your fucking father!"

Fuck wrong with this youngin? He thought.

This was the last thing he needed.

Stanley looked into his pupils. He could see the tiny red veins in his eyes and his heart pumped. "Nothing is wrong I just want—,"

"What? Me to be your father?" He gave him the slow glare from the top of his head to the bottom of his feet and back. He rocked slowly. "You lucky you not on your knees sucking my dick right now, young boy." He gripped his stick. "What would make you think even if you were my blood that I would have you as a son? A fucking snitch? Naw, homie, you could never have my last name." Rasim pushed him with both hands so hard he bounced against the wall.

If Rasim was acting, he was doing a good got damn job.

Stanley ran out of the room and Rasim was about to follow him because he didn't allow him to go anyplace without him. But his body was so heavy with the loss of Snow that he flopped to the bed instead.

"Want me to go after him?" Parker leaned his head in and asked.

Rasim threw his face into his hands. "No. Let him rock out."

Parker nodded and held the line.

The visiting hall was bustling thanks to Mindy's miraculous change of heart. More attractive women were allowed to meet with their loved ones and it was all because Snow orchestrated the proper beat down. When the battered C.O. returned, she decided to retire her hating ways. The last thing she wanted was to see a wolf sighting again. The females put more damage on her body than she could stand. Mindy knew she couldn't take another bout in the hospital.

Rasim was sitting in a plastic orange chair next to Queen but he might as well had stayed in his room. He was hunched over and staring out into the visiting hall at nothing in particular. Ironically, he did bear an amazing resemblance to the jeans Snow threw on the floor in her shop that day.

No movement.

No life.

Snow knew her husband. That was for sure.

PRISON THRONE

"Rasim, are you okay?" Queen asked frustrated at not receiving any attention.

Rasim did not hear a word she said.

"Rasim," she said louder, "are you okay?"

Rasim flapped his eyelids and turned around to face her. "Let me ask you something." He pointed at her and his finger brushed against her nose. "You sure you didn't tell my wife about us?" he glared. "Because I would kill you if you did. You do know that, right?"

Queen sat back in the hard plastic seat and folded her arms over her breasts. She was trying to be strong but her ass cheeks were clamped together to prevent from shitting in her thong. "Why do you keep asking me about that?" she frowned. "I'm sick of coming down here every week to see you only to not be appreciated." She stared directly into his eyes. "If you keep this up, I'm not coming back anymore."

"Did you tell my wife about us?" he repeated, fully expecting the right answer.

"No, Rasim," she said with her tongue fluttering around again. It was obvious that she was not on his mind. "But I do know she's moved on."

She turned away from him, thinking the matter was over when he gripped her arm, reducing the blood pressure in that particular limb.

"Nami!" Officer House yelled from across the room. "Hands off of that visitor!"

He slowly peeled his hands off of her flesh.

"Another move like that and the visit is over," he continued.

Rasim didn't give a fuck. He wanted this bitch to clarify her statement and after that she could go about her skanky way. "Queen, what do you mean she's moved on?"

"Rasim, I don't want to get involved—"

"Bitch, you already involved," he yelled. "Now what the fuck you talking 'bout?"

Queen knew that if she didn't give him the full story he could care less about the C.O. and would place his palms around her neck. By the time the officers got to him, her beating heart would be break dancing on the floor. "I don't know much." She shrugged. "I will say that she's moving in with some dude she met a while back. That's all I know."

A while back?

What the fuck?

Half of Rasim wanted to cry and the other half wanted to die. His wife, his precious wife was with another man and he couldn't fathom it in his mind. It was like reading a book full of Chinese script. He simply wasn't fluent in that particular language.

How was it possible for Snow...innocent Snow...to authorize another man to touch her body, to kiss her lips, to hold her when she knew full well that she belonged to him? It was like the nigga robbed him at gunpoint. What type of bullshit was that?

Rasim moved uneasily in his seat and stood up. He didn't want to talk to that bitch anymore. It wasn't personal; it was just cold hard facts. What they had was over anyway. It wasn't like he could fuck her.

So he strutted to the C.O. and said, "I'm ready to go back to my cell."

"Well you have to wait. It's not—"

Rasim cut him off with a cold glare. Either he walked him back to the block or he would hurt somebody or something to get a rougher escort. At any rate, the visit was over.

PRISON THRONE

Officer House knew when a prisoner was on the verge of a breakdown and he didn't want to taunt him and showcase his authority. Rasim was a respectful man. So he escorted him to his block without confrontation.

Rasim didn't give Queen the common courtesy of even saying goodbye. He couldn't even remember what she was wearing. It was as if she were never there. As if she never existed.

Unfortunately for Rasim, when he made it back to his cell he was awarded with more bad news.

Shawn and Parker slowly walked into his cell. Shawn opened his mouth to talk to Rasim but the words wouldn't come out, so he turned around and hung in the doorway instead.

Parker looked back at his friend and then at Rasim. He realized it was up to him to bear the cross alone. "Rasim, I gotta talk to you, man."

"What's up?" he asked with wide eyes. He could tell whatever it was it was going to be bad.

"Some nigga name Terry stabbed Stanley an hour ago," he whispered. "He said he looked like you. Like the last time he saw your face when you killed some nigga name Levi."

"Where is my son?" Rasim roared.

"In the infirmary. They saying he might not make it."

Rasim hung in front of the mosque within the prison. He wanted to walk inside and ask Allah for help but he didn't know how. Where would he start? He never bothered to rap to Him before.

BY T. STYLES

An older Muslim saw Rasim pacing and stood up and reached out his hand to pull him in. Rasim was so broken down that his legs could barely move so he could use the help. So much happened in his life that he realized he couldn't do it alone. It was out of his hands. It was time to surrender.

"How can I help you, young brother?" the man asked, seeing the despair on his face.

He was an old black man with a baldhead and bushy grey eyebrows. He turned his life over to Allah ten years ago when he accidently killed a child. He had been doing time and God's work ever since.

"I just need...I just need to pray." His voice was so high pitched it was cracking.

"Would you like my help?"

Rasim nodded.

"I take it you want to ask for Allah's assistance in your life?"

Rasim nodded again.

"Okay, you're going to prostrate by placing your forehead on the ground to show humility and submission before Allah." He paused and eased on his knees to demonstrate. "Come down here, young man. Let me show you."

Rasim eased down.

"Good. Now place your hands on the floor and then your forehead."

Rasim followed instructions like a G.

"Good. Now repeat after me. *Glory be to my Lord, the most High.*"

Rasim repeated the precious words.

"Okay now I'm going to give you some privacy. I want you to take the time to ask Allah for what troubles your soul. And when you're done, sit on your legs for a few seconds and prostrate again. Allah will hear your call. He always does."

The man eased out of the mosque and left him alone.

Rasim was grateful because his heart was heavy and he was too embarrassed to hold an audience and talk to Allah at the same time. Anyway, he felt like a hypocrite asking for God's grace considering all of the murders he facilitated but what else could he do? He tried his way and in the end he lost his wife and possibly his only son. He couldn't take any more.

For some reason, he thought about what Snow said when they were teenagers many years ago in Strawberry Meadows.

"You shouldn't turn your back on God, Rasim. You never know when you might need him."

He hoped it wasn't too late.

"Allah, I'm coming to You humbly. I know You don't recognize my face but I need Your help. I…I love my wife more than anything in this world. And I've made some mistakes, most of which I don't want to admit to, but I'm truly sorry. But I can't be the man I know I can be without her in my life. Please bring her back to me. Please give me the strength and help to be the husband she wants and deserves. Please help my son so that he doesn't die because of my sins. All I'm asking is a chance to be a good father. To be a good husband. To be a good man. I'm asking for Your mercy."

Rasim rose up for a few seconds and prostrated again.

When he was preparing to stand up and leave, Parker came into the mosque and whispered, "I'm sorry to bother

BY T. STYLES

you, Rasim. But your counselor said your wife is waiting on your call."

Rasim held the phone to his ear so close it almost muffled out her sweet voice. Just hearing her talk was like music to his ears. He figured Allah was great but he never expected Him to move so quickly. "Where you been, baby? I haven't spoken to you in months." It's funny how absence made his voice softer. The last time he spoke to her, he was yelling but now his tone was gentle as a baby's kiss.

"I've been out, Rasim," she responded in that breathy tone she was known for. "Where else would I be?"

He recognized how she was using his words against him but he didn't appreciate the humor. "What is that supposed to mean?" he asked pacing in the place in front of the phone booth.

"Listen, I didn't call to argue with you. I reached out because I heard what happened to your son. I know you wanted to help and I hate that the past affected his future. What happened to the man who hurt him anyway?"

Rasim didn't want to talk about that bullshit but he didn't want to be ignorant either. "He locked down. They're taking him to another prison later." He wanted to say that wherever he landed his reach was long enough to touch him but of course the call was recorded.

"That's good to hear," she replied knowing full well that he had plans to lay the stabber to rest. He should've bucked them all on the day he busted Levi. "So how is Stanley now?"

PRISON THRONE

"In critical condition," he sighed. "This is what I was talking about, baby. This is why I didn't want no kids. They fuckin' used him against me." Rasim paused realizing he was saying too much over the phone. "Anyway, I'm hoping for the best. How did you find out?"

"Selena. She was bouncing off the walls too. Said something about Stanley having a fractured jaw and now this."

Rasim rubbed his temple. "Selena, need to back the fuck up and relax." Rasim leaned up against the wall and looked up at the light. He had another question, although he wasn't sure if he was prepared for the answer. "Snow, are you...are you dealing with another nigga?"

She exhaled. "Do you really want to know the answer to that question?"

His guts bubbled even more. "Yeah."

"Yes I am."

Rasim lost all reason and religion.

He pushed off the wall and yelled, "But why?" He startled a few inmates who were already terrified of him as they walked by. They hustled down the hall before they gained a fractured jaw like Stanley or suffered dying in their sleep like Montana. "What would make you do some shit like that, Snow? You've never been with another man outside of me. Not every nigga is gonna respect your body like I do, baby. You gotta be careful."

"Who said I never been with another man but you?"

Rasim was as stiff as his first hard on. "So...so you...you saying before I came back in here that you were with another nigga? Outside of me?"

"Yes."

His free hand crawled into a fist and he pumped it repeatedly like he was about to give blood. "Who the nigga, Snow?"

"Rasim, please don't—"

"Who?" he roared.

"Somebody from Strawberry Meadows."

Rasim touched his stomach. "When, Snow?" he yelled. "What the fuck you doing to me? You want me to zap out on these niggas in here? And get ten to twenty?" he paused. "Huh?"

Hearing his statement an inmate who was on the phone next to him immediately hung up on his mother. The old woman was in the hospital and everything. But the last thing he needed was to be a victim of Rasim's wrath so he bounced.

"I was with him the last time I left you," she responded. "When I was gone all of those months and came home to find you on the floor under the sink with blood pouring out of your head. After you put a rock to your face." She paused. "He took care of me then and he's taking care of me now."

Every vein in Rasim's body pulsed and bubbled. "So when you left me you were living with another man the entire time?"

"Yes."

"Why didn't you tell me?"

"You didn't ask." She paused. "Don't be so surprised, Rasim."

"Just because I fucked some bitch? You would go this far?"

"That's what's wrong in our marriage. I caught you letting another female suck your dick and I decided I wouldn't take it anymore. Do you remember that? Just be-

PRISON THRONE

cause you're a nigga don't mean you can be unfaithful, Rasim. I deserve more." She paused. "What did you think," she giggled, "just because I was quiet that another man wouldn't look at me? Huh? Did you really think I was that undesirable?" If that wasn't enough, she took jabs at his jugular. "Didn't you notice the next time we made love how my fuck game gained value? He taught me and he's going to teach me so much more."

Rasim was so hot you could fry a bag of nuggets on his forehead. He licked his lips and then wiped them with the back of his hands. "Snow, when I see you I'm going to choke the life out of your pretty face. Then we'll see if your nigga will still want you when your body is blue."

"You have to get out of jail first."

Click.

Rasim was on his bunk with his hand behind his head and the other tucked in his pants.

He was planning his wife's bloody murder.

Rasim spoke to Snow over a month ago and he hadn't heard from her since. The only bright side in the tunnel is that Stanley was getting better. Because of his fractured jaw and the recent stabbing, they decided to keep him segregated from the rest of the population until his sentence as over. Rasim preferred it that way because at least he would know that he was safe.

He started to write Snow another hate letter but the next thing that happened fucked up his head. Officer House strolled into his cell and said, "Nami, it's time to go."

Rasim looked up to him from the bunk. "What you mean?"

"You're being released."

He tilted his head. "Being released? I got at least five left."

"They're letting you go now, man. We need the space so they reduced your sentence."

Rasim grinned.

Imagine his luck.

Suddenly it was payback time.

Rasim's eyes were as wide as the windshield as he drove in his Escalade on the way to his house. It had been seven months since he laid eyes on his wife and it was time.

When he was released earlier in the day, Brooklyn and Chance picked him up. They made several attempts to calm him down by getting some drinks up in him or maybe a good meal but Rasim wouldn't hear none of it. He had a one-track mind and all he wanted was to see Snow.

Yes, he was anxious to get his palms around her neck. She violated severely when she told him that she fucked another man. He knew he was wrong considering he had many, including Selena and Queen, her sworn enemies.

But it was different for men. They had the right of the land and that included the women who grazed upon it and he needed a variety to survive. If he recalled correctly, even Jesus said that. Right? If Snow didn't see it his way then that was fine with him. He would simply choke her until she realized it.

Damn. Because of Snow, he was going to break his vow to never touch a woman. Unfortunately it wasn't the first vow he broke; he started with his marriage of course.

When he pulled up on his block he saw two cars parked out front of his house. One belonged to Snow and the other God only knew. In his haste the last time he spoke to her he forgot to ask the name of the person in Strawberry Meadows she fucked.

Had he been given the name he would've started with him and then worked his way to her. He only hoped that the violator wasn't close to him, like somebody he loved.

Rasim parked his ride and hustled toward his house. He was about to use his key but when he turned the knob, he immediately gained entry. Who he saw next caused his blood to boil over. The perpetrator was wearing a high-end security officer uniform complete with a shiny gold badge and stripes on his shoulder. He was standing on a chair in the middle of the living room removing a light bulb.

Seeing his angry face, the Security Guard hopped off of the chair in an attempt to run. But Rasim rushed inside, gripped him by the collar and slammed him into a beautiful crystal vase that sat on a small table by the door. Not done with him quite yet, he crashed his body through the glass table before stealing him in the jaw. With thoughts of him fucking his wife fresh in his mind, Rasim picked him up, carried him over to the window and pushed him through it before pressing him through the window on the right too. Both fractured under the weight of his body as glass splashed to the floor and cut into his face.

Rasim was so focused that he didn't see the gun on the Security Guard's belt until it was brushing against his nostrils. The matter had escalated quickly and in an attempt to save his own life Rasim stole him in the eye and knocked the weapon out of his hand.

But the Security Officer hustled toward his weapon and with him unarmed momentarily, Rasim dipped toward the basement to grab his .45.

Unfortunately he wasn't alone. Ole boy was right behind him.

The Security Guard fired in Rasim's direction, sending bullets screaming past his head and into another window. Luckily Rasim was faster and was able to pull the basement door open moments before another bullet went flying into the wood paneling of the door.

Once inside, Rasim closed and locked it and dodged down the steps toward his safe. Quickly he keyed in the code, grabbed his gun and loaded it with bullets. To be sure he had enough, he also stuffed ammo into his pockets and slowly crept back upstairs.

From inside the basement, before opening the door, he could hear his wife yelling but he couldn't make out her words. All that did was cause his blood to boil over as he pushed out of the basement, armed and ready. For all he knew, the nigga got fly and decided to take his frustrations out on Snow and he wasn't having it. Not while he was home. Not while he was alive.

Creeping out of the basement, he maintained his aim. Slowly he advanced toward the living room and that's when he saw him. At the top of the foyer holding Snow's hand as if they were leaving together.

Fuck they think they going?

Snow stared into Rasim's eyes but then she looked away as if she were trying to hold back her feelings. It had been months since she'd seen him and look at what had become of their marriage.

Over the decades, their love had grown together, each being the other's first sexual experience and yet Snow was essentially saying she was going to be with another man and that she didn't want him anymore.

Picture that shit.

"Snow, what you doing? Why you even with this clown?"

The Security Officer assumed he wouldn't fire if he had his wife with him, which was why he didn't shoot at Rasim either. "We leaving, Rasim." The Security Officer said. "Just put the gun down. You don't want to hurt Snow and we don't want trouble. All we want is to go about our life."

He would've been better off not saying a word. Angry beyond belief at how he held his wife's hand like she belonged to him, Rasim fired at the Security Officer and caught him in the meaty part of his thigh. "What the fuck?" he yelled as the gun dropped and toppled out of his hand. "You fucking shot me!" He leaned against the wall and dropped.

"Rasim, what are you doing?" Snow screamed with her hands covering her mouth when she saw him fall. "It's over! Just leave me the fuck alone! You trying to go back to jail? Huh?"

"Snow, get the fuck back in the room," Rasim demanded. When she didn't move he said, "I'm not fucking around with you. You don't want to test my limits right now. Trust me."

Realizing there was no reasoning with him, she dipped into their bedroom and waited for whatever happened next. Little did she know, her husband was just getting started.

Quick visions of their sexual exploits whipped through Rasim's mind again as he crept up the steps. His plan was to kill him, nothing more and nothing less. When Rasim was standing over him, the Security Officer yelled, "What the fuck is wrong with you? What are you some type of terrorist?" he said taking jabs at his race.

With the windows open, Rasim's nosey next-door neighbor Bridget heard the words she always knew were true. That the Nami family was involved in terrorism and now she had proof. She saw the security guard walk Snow in earlier and figured he said it. Feeling validated, she rushed inside to make a call with the proper remix of course. In her story a cop was involved and a member of Al-Qaeda.

From inside of the home, the Security Officer yelled, "Please don't shoot me again, man. I don't want to die."

But there was no use. Rasim knew he had been with his wife and he would never be able to live knowing that he was walking around in the world. So he fired into his chest and watched his eyes as they widened before closing.

In all of the commotion, he didn't realize that the outside of his home was suddenly flooded with SWAT vehicles. When Rasim saw the police moving toward the house, he dragged the Security Guard's body in front of the middle door. He wanted to hold him for ransom. Just in case.

Afterward, he tried to go into the bedroom with Snow but she locked it shut. "Open the door, Snow!" he yelled. "Since I'm going back to jail, we have to talk."

"No!" she responded. "Stay the fuck away from me! You have gone too far now and I don't trust you."

PRISON THRONE

Rasim glanced behind him out of the broken window downstairs and saw more officers approaching. He wanted to talk to her alone before he was taken and arrested. It may be the last time they would ever get. "Snow, please! I won't hurt you. Just give me a few minutes."

"Stay the fuck away from me, Rasim. I'm serious."

Frustrated, Rasim hustled into the guest room and waited. The moment he locked the door, the house phone rang. Reluctantly he sat the gun on the bed and walked over to it. He picked up the phone and placed it against his ear. "Are you in charge?" an officer questioned.

Rasim shook his head in disbelief. His entire life was over now and he knew it. He sat on the edge of the bed. Sighed and said, "Yes."

"My name is Alf Herman and I was told that a man was shot inside of your home," he spoke calmly. "Can we send someone in to get him?"

"No." he paused. "Not unless I tell you my story."

"Okay, we can do that down at the station."

"No." He paused. "In my home and on my terms. That's the only way I'm letting him go."

CHAPTER 23

MAY 2014
WASHINGTON, DC

PRESENT DAY

Alf Herman was stunned silent as he sat in his chair with his eyes glued on the door. Although Rasim and Snow did a supreme job of storytelling, they purposely avoided anything pertaining to murders or their drug crimes. In the end, most of their fabrication involved Rasim and the many women who loved him.

Because he couldn't talk about his father without hurting, he even left out the suicide. Rasim mentioned the story of his father's death as if he was murdered in a gun accident.

Even the narrative about Rasim reentering prison received a final cut. The only thing Alf was told was that he went to prison with one mission in mind, to help his son and that he never meant to lose his wife in the process. Nothing about the fractured jaw or the murder.

There was one other detail omitted since Rasim's story stopped at him receiving the surprise for an early release while still in prison. Who was the gentleman lying on the floor with blood pooling out of his body?

"I heard your stories. But can you tell me his name?" he called out.

"His name is Southeast Brian Goodwin," Rasim said through clenched teeth. "He was with us at Strawberry Meadows. That's how she met him," he said with hate in his voice.

Brian had been there all along.

When she was crying in the Movie Room, the day Rasim swung her panties around in the air at the home, Brian tried to console her when she sat on the couch but she said to leave her alone. When she cleaned Rasim's bed and folded his clothes, Brian told her that Rasim was using her but she said to leave her alone. When she and Rasim played Spades together for the first time, Brian was in the corner hating with his boys. And the day she left the center, due to catching Rasim telling his friends about how he fucked Selena, Brian, who was leaving on a pass, asked Snow if she wanted a ride. This time she said yes.

Southeast Brian had been there all the time lying in wait for Rasim to fuck up but in his arrogance, Rasim never noticed.

Alf exhaled because Southeast Brian was a civilian. At least he was not an officer. It wasn't like he felt comfortable turning around and calling off the SWAT team either. But realizing blue blood wasn't spilling on the floor upstairs brought him a little relief.

In the hopes of saving the man's life it was time to play the last card. "Rasim, I haven't been totally honest about who I am."

"Meaning?" he yelled.

"Before coming I pulled your sheet," Alf responded gaining authority and momentum. "I know you aren't the kind of man people think you are. You aren't a terrorist."

"You don't know shit about me," he yelled.

"I know a lot about you," he said confidently. "Including some things you didn't share with me in your story. I know that your father killed himself, believing that he betrayed Al-Qaeda for not participating in the terrorist attacks of 9/11. I know that he loved you very much and his decision to commit suicide changed the course of your life forever. And I know that you are a good man trapped in a bad situation."

Silence.

"Rasim, may I bring in someone who has been waiting patiently to talk to you for years?"

Originally he was going to say no but he was going to jail anyway. So what did he have to lose? "Is it another cop? 'Cause there's one cop too many in here right now if you ask me."

"He's not a cop," Alf responded honestly. "Please trust me."

At that time, Rasim heard a slight Urdu accent that wasn't present before. Had he hidden it the entire time? If so, why?

"Go ahead. I'm waiting."

Alf waved outside and instructed the visitor to come in. Although Rasim remained behind the door, he wanted to know who was so important in his home.

"Rasim, may I see you?" the man yelled to the doors.

When he finally heard the voice of a man very familiar, his muscles weakened and he dropped to the bed.

"Rasim, please, I would like to talk to you. Come to me now."

Horrified that he may be hearing things, Rasim opened the bedroom door at a snail's pace. When he dawdled toward the banister and looked down, just as he thought, he was staring into his father's face.

But how? The last time he saw his corpse was at the funeral. He watched them sit him into the ground.

And then he remembered something important. He didn't know much because it hurt Rasim's father too much to talk about. Rasim's father, Kamran, had a twin brother who married rich and his name was Vazir. Could that be him?

Rasim gripped the banister unarmed and looked down. Southeast Brian's body lay at his feet. "What…how…?"

"Son, I need you to come down here right now!" Vazir roared raising his hand for him to hold. "I need you to look me in the eyes and tell me what is going on. Come now, Rasim!"

Rasim's body wanted to obey the man with his father's features but he couldn't move. After all, he stood as tall as his father, which forced automatic respect to enter his heart. And then suddenly he grew angry. "How could you abandon your own brother?" he yelled remembering bits of the story Kamran told him briefly. "If you were in his life, he may still be alive today. He may be with me now."

Vazir looked down at his hands and stuffed them into his pockets. "You're right. If I had been in my brother's life, and yours, he may still be alive." He paused for a moment. "And this may not have been your fate. Trust me, son, I grapple with the fact that my family was destroyed every day. But I married a woman who I didn't love for money. In exchange for financial freedom for myself and my brother so that he could have the proper schooling in computer technology. When she died due to complications,

I came to America to reunite with your father but he refused to see me. I even brought my son, his nephew, to meet him but still he declined and I never got a chance to see him. My son is your cousin. Who stands right here." He pointed at Alf Herman or as his full name dictated, Alf Herman Nami.

Rasim trembled.

Snow wanted to open the door to lay eyes on the men who were her husband's blood. But she decided against it.

"Are you saying that this cop is my cousin?" Rasim asked looking at him.

Vazir nodded.

Rasim shook his head and wiped his hand down his face. "But why like this? Why are you meeting me now?"

"I've been in the country for thirty years. But Kamran, for fear of your emotional safety, forced me to stay away. I respected my brother's wishes even though I visited you as often as I could in secrecy. However, you spotted me a few times, after his death. Although I don't think you believed I was real."

"What do you mean?"

"I was at the funeral. I was there when you married your beautiful wife. I was there when you were coming out of a body shop recently. I have always been there."

Rasim remembered seeing his father at various times but he thought his mind was playing tricks on him, which was one of the reasons he gave up liquor and weed.

Vazir looked at Southeast Brian who was not moving. "Rasim, come. Come now and end this. Do not put another blemish on our people in a country I know you love. Please."

PRISON THRONE

Ashamed, Rasim gripped at the banister and slowly he crept down the stairs until he was eye-to-eye with the man who looked like his father.

Vazir gripped Rasim and hugged him tightly. It was only for a second because SWAT rushed in and brought Rasim to his knees. His face was pressed against the broken glass as handcuffs were slapped on his wrists. When they had a hold of him, they yanked him up roughly. This shit took too long and they were irritated.

Rasim observed Alf who looked so much like him they could be brothers. He reasoned that he was a member of a family with strong genes.

It was a coincidence that Alf was a member of the police department and it was as if the Universe had conspired to reunite the family when he got the call about the terrorist attack at that address. When he heard Rasim's name over the radio, he contacted his father for help, got approval from the higher ups and invited him down.

Maybe, just maybe, Rasim's prayers in the mosque in prison that day came true. He remembered a part of his prayer clearly.

"Please give me the strength and help to be the husband she wants and deserves."

Was this the help Allah had given?

"Can you tell my wife I'm sorry?" Rasim asked looking at his uncle and then Alf. "Can you tell her I love her no matter what?"

Vazir nodded. "I will, son. And I'll see you soon. We both will."

BY T. STYLES

Rasim stood next to his attorney and awaited the verdict. The past six months had been a long road and he was eager for it to be over, whether the judgment be in his favor or not.

As he peeped the view behind him, he was disappointed that throughout the trial Snow hadn't bothered to show her face. Not one time. She made a decision to leave him alone and she stood by it. The agony of losing her worsened since he sat in the cell with nothing but a fat chunk of time on his hands.

However dark it got, and it was bleak, there was somehow a brighter side. Rasim grew closer to his uncle Vazir, his cousin Alf and Stanley. Vazir and Alf visited regularly and he learned so much about Pakistani tradition. Kamran had been willing to teach him too but it's amazing how losing his father made Rasim appreciate his heritage and people even more.

And then there was his son. A month after he was arrested, Stanley was released. They talked about their time together in prison and Rasim tried to make amends. But Stanley was different. The innocence in Stanley's heart was stolen and Rasim would need to leave prison to repair the bond. It would take work but it was a job he was willing to take.

Although Rasim looked to Allah for more help these days, he was still an ordinary man. Just like a child to his parents, there would be times where Rasim would follow the law but many more times where he would be disobedient.

With that said, he sent a prison kite (contraband letter with specific instructions hidden in its pages) to Chance and Brooklyn to pay a willing convict to kill Terry and a wolf to kill Queen. Both executions were processed and completed.

After speaking to Parker and Shawn through another prison kite, Rasim learned how Mindy and Queen conspired to keep him from his wife by denying her visitation. He added one and one together and realized she was probably the reason Snow abandoned him too. It enraged him that he allowed her into his life.

"Jury, have you reached a verdict?" Judge Edward Tomlin asked.

"Yes, Your Honor, we have," said the juror with the wild curly fro.

"What say you?"

"We the people find Rasim Nami not guilty," the woman smiled looking at Rasim, knowing he would appreciate the good news.

Rasim leaned in, almost not believing his ears. He looked over to his left at his attorney who placed one hand on his shoulder while the other gripped his hand in a firm shake. "You're free."

Rasim exhaled in disbelief.

Six months ago it looked as if Rasim was a shoe in for a timeshare in the Federal Prison system but the prosecution had one hurdle to overcome. There was no way to convict him properly when Southeast Brian, who almost died after suffering a collapsed lung, testified in Rasim's favor.

It was virtually impossible to convict a man on an attempted murder charge when the victim claimed that he was shot by another shooter before he walked into the house. Of course it was ridiculous but Brian was so serious when he was on the stand that they had no choice but to believe him.

BY T. STYLES

It also didn't hurt that while Snow was telling Alf her version of the story, when they were in the house, Rasim successfully scrubbed all of the gunpowder residue off of his hands with bleach in the guest bathroom. He also removed the bullets from his pocket and his prints off of the weapon.

The prosecution was annoyed because they hadn't counted on Southeast Brian's betrayal.

What man wouldn't want justice?

Even if Rasim hadn't sent Brooklyn and Chance to his hospital with a get well soon card and wide eyes filled with future threats to Southeast Brian, he had no intentions on helping the state. His reason didn't involve Rasim's power or the quiet visits from his compadres. It was because although he owned a reputable business, he was still a man of the streets and there was a code.

Besides, Snow made it clear after the ordeal that it would be best if they went their separate ways so there was nothing left to fight for. He didn't even get the girl. Southeast Brian didn't buck much, seeing as how her husband slumped his lungs and all.

After winning his case, Rasim hugged his well-paid counselors, uncle, cousin and son and the party was over. He told Chance and Brooklyn that he would meet them later for drinks because he wanted a few moments alone.

After being processed for release, Rasim slipped on his coat and dipped out of the courtroom. He moved down the hall, out of the building and away from the reporters with too much makeup on their faces and intimidating mics in their hands.

It snowed earlier so his boots crunched against the ice as he made his exit. November was certainly chilly but he didn't mind, at least he was free.

PRISON THRONE

Six blocks later he was still alone with the sounds of tires driving over the damp street. His thoughts kept him company until a beautiful woman with eyes as brown as caramel candies pulled up on him blasting Mary J. Blige's voice through her speakers.

♪ "You're all...I need...to get by.♪

♪You're all...I need...to get by," ♪ Mary sang.

Wow. It was Snow.

Rasim blinked a few times because this could not be real. If it were an evil joke, he would not be able to survive afterwards.

But if it was real...if she was really there, what a beautiful way to heal his broken heart.

Snow, who looked like the six months had been very kind to her, turned the music down and said, "Need a lift?"

Rasim tried to be smooth but you have to understand. He dreamed about this woman every day for the past six months. She was his life. She was his everything. So he threw coolness to the wind, rushed to the car and slid inside before she could change her mind.

The brightness of her smile and the warmth of the heater running made him feel instantly at home. "Hello, Rasim," she whispered.

Rasim turned his body so that he faced her. He touched her face with the back of his hand. He battled with feelings of anger and love. "Why did you do me like this?" he asked softly. "Huh?" His hand dropped. "I almost killed a nigga fucking with you."

"I should be asking you the same thing."

He frowned. "How you figure?"

"I have taken care of you all of my young life. I bathed you. I fed you and I loved you even when it was difficult. All I asked was that you protect my heart and you failed."

"So you go fuck another nigga instead?" he roared.

"No," she whispered shaking her head, as a tear rolled down her face. "So I go and try to be happy, Rasim. Don't you see that? All I wanted to do was love you. But you couldn't love me the way I deserved." She wiped the tears away with her fingertips.

Rasim turned around in his seat and focused on traffic to control his thoughts. "But the nigga was in your body, baby. Moving around and shit. Making you...I mean...Why?" He couldn't verbalize it. It was like a horror movie.

"You're worrying about what doesn't matter. Sex." She paused. "You of all people should know that."

"Don't be smart, Snow," he said in a frustrated tone.

"I'm serious. You should not have been cheating in the first place, Rasim. You doing all this shit behind my back when you didn't even ask me if I was with the shit."

He turned around to face her. "With what?"

"I've never been with a woman but I realize things get dry sometimes in relationships. I really do. We've been together for over fourteen years, Rasim! Come to me and tell me you're thinking about wanting something new and let's pick someone together. If that's what you want. But you don't have me running around DC like I'm queen when lesser bitches have slept with my husband." Rasim grew silent. "At the end of the day, you were scared to come to me and that's weak on your part."

"I ain't no weak man, Snow!"

"And I never said you were," she said softly. "I said the move you made was weak because you should have toughened up and been real with me."

PRISON THRONE

"But that bitch didn't mean anything to me!"

"Then why are we here? Why were you locked up?" She paused. "You're always talking about running intel on niggas when you forgot to run it on your whore." Snow tilted her body and leaned against the window. "She didn't want your dick, Rasim. She wanted my position and you operated as if it were a possibility."

Rasim rubbed his throbbing temples. She was right but he was still stressed.

"You're so worried about sitting on the throne that you forgot about your queen," she continued. "How could you?"

Now he was angry. "I never forgot about you, Snow. Ever! I put it down to that bitch what it was from the jump. She just neglected to play her position that's all."

He appreciated Snow's independence and all but he was worried that she would act differently. He loved submissive Snow. But he wasn't sure about this new independent bitch. Rasim needed to be with a woman who needed him, who could follow his lead. Every man did.

"I know the new me is a little uncomfortable for you," Snow continued as if she could read his thoughts. "I can see it in your eyes. Just because I speak my mind doesn't mean I don't love you or that I'm not willing to follow. I'm stronger now and I have you to thank." She touched his hand. "Anyway, why would you want a lesser woman by your side? You run an empire with your strongest, never with the weaker. So if you're my king, rule! And I will humble myself and follow your lead. Always."

He looked into her eyes again. "You know I'm coming back home, right?"

She grinned. "What you thought I was here for my health?" she giggled. "Dinner is already on the table.

BY T. STYLES

Brooklyn, Chance and the twins are at the house waiting on you and everything. I called Vazir and Alf and asked them to come too, along with Stanley."

"Who cooked?" he grinned.

"Mute Candy. And yes she made your favorite fried chicken."

His stomach grumbled in anticipation. He looked outside again at the powder falling from the sky. "If I ever find out you fucked another nigga, I will kill you, Snow." He focused on her with serious intent. "I hope you can understand that."

"Then I guess we'll be doused in blood. Because if you step out on me again, I can't make any promises."

He looked her over. Damn she was beautiful. "You looking good, baby."

She observed her jeans, identified a few flaws and sighed. "I'm not going to lie, I don't feel my best anymore." She ran her hands over her thighs.

"I can't tell."

"I'm serious, Rasim. When you looked at me I felt your love. I felt sexy." She grew serious. "And now I don't anymore. I miss that."

"Yeah, you right." He nodded. "Now that I think about it you do look a little fat."

Snow felt gut punched and she lowered her head. "Damn."

"In all the right places, that is."

She looked into his eyes and smiled.

"Make time to laugh at the dumb shit. Besides, even with that flat butt, with a face like yours you still a ten." They both giggled remembering the Strawberry Meadows days. "Say my name," Rasim continued.

With a wide smile she whispered, "Rasim."

PRISON THRONE

He rubbed her face again and softly pinched her chin. "I love you, Snow."

"I love you, Rasim." She paused. "And you can have sex with me if you want."

He chuckled harder remembering the first day they made love. "Snow, when we get in that house I'm breaking down walls in that pussy." He gripped his dick. "Just so you know."

"Then let me take you home so we can eat and get them niggas out of our house," she winked.

"I'm with you, Mrs. Rasim Nami. Let's roll."

And it was just like that.

Just like it was in the Strawberry Meadows days, if we're being honest.

Snow Bradshaw, Rasim's God sent angel, had made the decision to save his life.

Again.

Reviews are like little love letters from readers.
Will you write to me?

-T. Styles

Would you like to be an author?

We are currently taking submissions.

Please email your COMPLETE manuscript to:
<u>*cartelpublications@yahoo.com.*</u>

Be sure to include the following: Name, contact number, available time and synopsis.

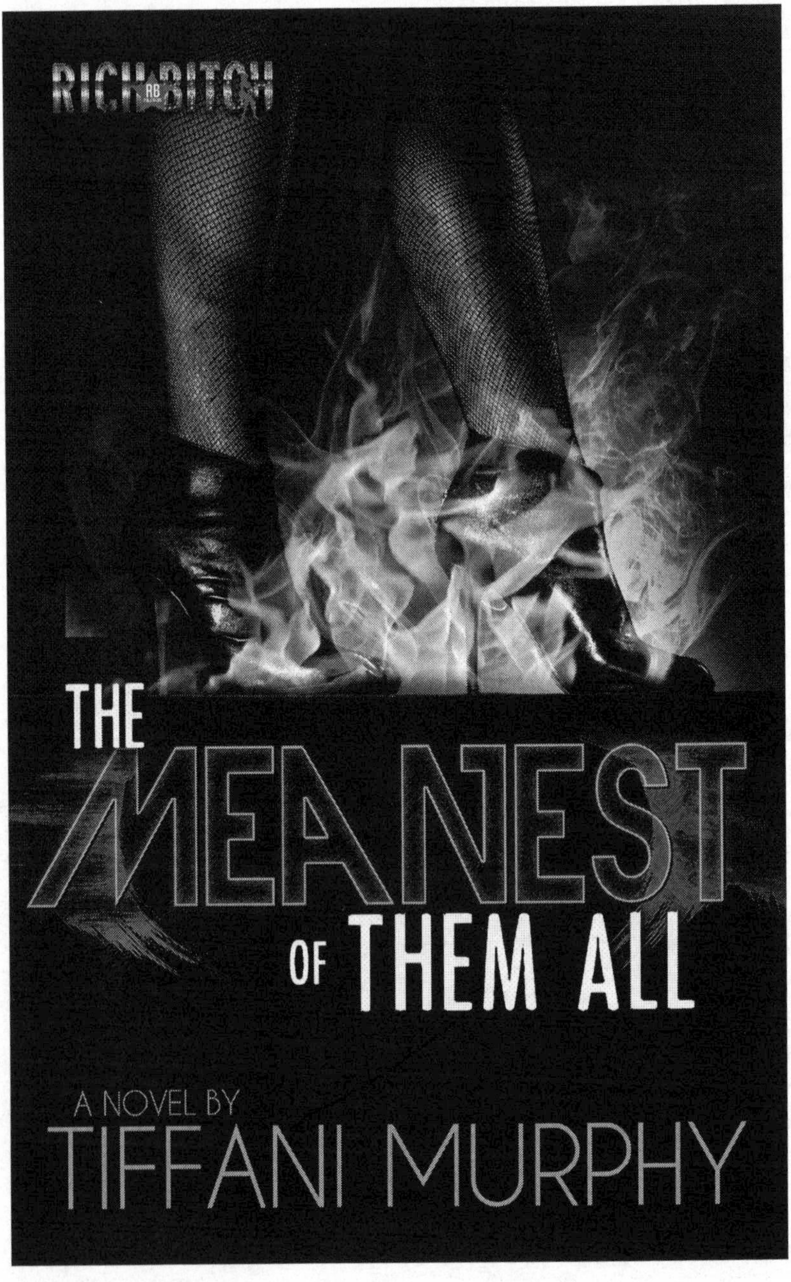
RICH BITCH
THE
MEANEST
OF THEM ALL
A NOVEL BY
TIFFANI MURPHY

GOON

T. STYLES

NATIONAL BEST SELLING AUTHOR OF *RAUNCHY*

The Cartel Collection
Established in January 2008
We're growing stronger by the month!!!
www.thecartelpublications.com

Cartel Publications Order Form
Inmates <u>ONLY</u> get novels for $10.00 per book!

Titles		*Fee*
Shyt List	_____	$15.00
Shyt List 2	_____	$15.00
Pitbulls In A Skirt	_____	$15.00
Pitbulls In A Skirt 2	_____	$15.00
Pitbulls In A Skirt 3	_____	$15.00
Pitbulls In A Skirt 4	_____	$15.00
Victoria's Secret	_____	$15.00
Poison	_____	$15.00
Poison 2	_____	$15.00
Hell Razor Honeys	_____	$15.00
Hell Razor Honeys 2	_____	$15.00
A Hustler's Son 2	_____	$15.00
Black And Ugly As Ever	_____	$15.00
Year of The Crack Mom	_____	$15.00
The Face That Launched a Thousand Bullets		
	_____	$15.00
The Unusual Suspects	_____	$15.00
Miss Wayne & The Queens of DC		
	_____	$15.00
Year of The Crack Mom	_____	$15.00
Paid in Blood	_____	$15.00
Shyt List III	_____	$15.00
Shyt List IV	_____	$15.00
Raunchy	_____	$15.00
Raunchy 2	_____	$15.00
Raunchy 3	_____	$15.00
Jealous Hearted	_____	$15.00
Quita's Dayscare Center	_____	$15.00
Quita's Dayscare Center 2	_____	$15.00
Shyt List V	_____	$15.00
Deadheads	_____	$15.00
Pretty Kings	_____	$15.00
Pretty Kings II	_____	$15.00
Drunk & Hot Girls	_____	$15.00
Hersband Material	_____	$15.00
Upscale Kittens	_____	$15.00
Wake & Bake Boys	_____	$15.00
Young & Dumb	_____	$15.00
Tranny 911	_____	$15.00
Tranny 911: Dixie's Rise	_____	$15.00
First Comes Love Then Comes Murder	_____	$15.00
Young & Dumb: Vyce's Getback	_____	$15.00
Luxury Tax	_____	$15.00
Mad Maxxx	_____	$15.00
The Lying King	_____	$15.00
Crazy Kind of Love	_____	$15.00
Silence of the Nine	_____	$15.00
Prison Throne	_____	$15.00

Please add $4.00 per book for shipping and handling.
The Cartel Publications * P.O. Box 486 * Owings Mills * MD * 21117

Name: _____

Address:_____

City/State:_____

Contact # & Email:_____

Please allow 5-7 business days for delivery. The Cartel is not responsible for prison orders rejected.

<u>Personal Checks Are Not Accepted.</u>